ALL THAT REMAINS

NICHOLAS SIZER

DEDICATION

This book is dedicated to everyone who has shown me support throughout this process. I hope you enjoy every word that you read and look forward to my next piece of work. I appreciate each and every one of you.

CONTENTS

ACKNOWLEDGMENTS

First and foremost, I want to thank everyone who gave this book a chance. I want you to be able to use your imagination as you read to fill in some of the details and visualize every word. I want to thank my Mother and Sister for all of their support. Ra for the push to finally get this done. Big plans coming. Kate for being my sneak preview reader and giving me your insight. Tai, it's finally done. We need to finish the ones we started and get those published…asap. Thank you everyone for the love and support.

Chapter One

The Adventure Begins

On a cool spring afternoon, in the hills of a secluded area of a small suburban town, a high school is letting out with their students running amok. The school itself is a typical six-story cookie cutout of a place, with a max capacity of 450 students, three outdoor basketball courts with a fence circling the entire building with an employee parking lot in the back with its own security keypad entrance. In a matter of seconds, the school grounds litter with students with not an inch of pavement to be seen, if one were to view the scene from above. Lining the curbs along the school, as if it were a giant banana boat, rows and rows of school buses await the children before they can depart on their long road home. Slowly and over time, the students start disappearing from around the school. As with any school, there are always students who always stick around for a couple minutes after class lets out.

One such student who has decided to hang out after school was over is William, a junior at the high school who decided to wait for his girlfriend by the corner of the school while leaning up against the fence. After a few minutes of thinking to himself and minding his own business, William overhears a conversation between two other students, whom of which he does not know personally and decides to listen in and gain some insight on the topic of discussion. These two other students appear to be freshmen at which William does not recognize in the least bit and is eager to listen in on their conversation.

Now, William is just like any other junior at this high school, a student who does not like doing his homework, a class clown but overall he is a good guy but sometimes tends to have a bit of a "me first" attitude. He is about five feet six inches, stocky, a large tribal dragon tattoo running down his right arm from his shoulder to mid forearm, close haircut, wearing blue cargo shorts with a blue designer shirt and blue sneakers and ankle socks, all to go along with a matching blue baseball hat and a trimmed goatee.

"You would not believe the stories I have heard about this house down in midtown. I thought I was the only one who knew about this place," the one chubby freshman says while he was sitting under the tree for shade at the far end of the school. As he looked more as if he was ready for a math convention or an after school study hall with a bit of that typical nerd appeal to his demeanor. He has big thick black glasses on with a blue and white checkered plaid shirt with shorts to match, white sneakers with his socks up to his calves rocking curly black hair.

"Oh yeah? What stories? And which house are you talking about?" asked the other freshman sitting on the ground next to the kid with the glasses. Dressed in tight blue jeans with barely enough room for his legs to bend, a white shirt with short sleeves, shoulder length black hair, while also wearing white sneakers more adapted to be a skater kid.

"Some house in midtown that is haunted by ghosts," says the curly haired kid while fixing his glasses.

"Yeah right. How dumb do you have to be to believe a story like that? Oh wait, I think I just answered my own question," said the other freshman while laughing at the curly haired kid.

"Screw you peanut almond head."

"Yeah yeah."

"Punk!"

"Right back at ya." Still laughing at the curly head kid.

"Anyway, this is a real story whether you choose to believe it or not," the curly head kid is now standing up under the tree and dusting off the back of his shorts. "Just because you don't believe something doesn't mean that it is not real."

"And yet, nobody has seen it on the news or in the papers. Yeah, real believable there buddy." Now playing with a stick that he just picked up and is starting to strip the bark off and flicking it towards the tree.

"Don't act like you're never heard of an urban legend."

"Yes. They are just that though, a legend. Passed down from who knows who from who knows where from. Any and everybody put a different spin on the story to make it sound that much better than the last version," the other freshman with the stick says in such a sarcastic tone.

"Sure, call it what you want," said the Curly head kid. "I'm telling you the truth. Ghosts appear and eerie sounds whistle all night long from that place."

William now seeming intrigued by the conversation going back and forth between the two freshmen decides to approach them and try to gain farther insight. "You say it's an urban legend huh or is this story just something that your parents made up to make sure you two were home when the street lights turned on?"

The two teens look up at William walking over with amazement in their eyes as to how some stranger who they do not know and have never seen before just decides to interfere in their personal conversation. The two start standing up next to each other not knowing what William's intrusion's true intent seems to be so they want to be ready for whatever he tries to bring to the table.

"And who might you be?" asked the Skater teen who is still a little leery of an approaching William.

"Calm down big dog. It is not even that serious. I just heard something of interest and wanted to hear a little more about the discussion you two were having," William explains while holding his hands up in the air, stopping under the tree in which the two teens are standing under. The two teens are looking at William dead in his eyes and are carefully watching for any sudden signs of movement so that they may have a chance to take off running away. "I'm not here to hurt either one of you. I just found your urban legend interesting that's all."

"And why do you feel that you have to interrupt a private conversation because you heard something that interest to you?" asked the Skater.

"Not that private if I can hear what you are saying. Especially when we are standing here in the open for the world to hear and see what's going on," replied William.

"Why bother adding your two cents to a conversation that does no concern you in the least bit," the Skater said with a little frustration in his voice.

William just laughs at little at the situation. "Aren't we a tad bit hostile today for no apparent reason?"

The Curly head kid makes his attempt to diffuse and calm the situation. "Calm down. Save that crap for another time and place. It is not even that serious for you to get all emotional."

The Skater kid is just starting to pace back and forth from the gate to the tree (no more than five feet between the two) trying hard not to say something controversial. Still in shock that his friend defended a stranger especially one of which neither of them personally know. He decides to sit back down under the tree to calm down and continues playing with the stick that he stripped the bark off earlier.

William nods to the Curly head kid. “Thank you.” Still in amazement, that he even uttered those words in the same sentence. “So a real haunted house huh? There is no way that can be true.”

“Don’t tell him anything! We don’t even know him.”

“Chill man,” the Curly head kid says towards the Skater. After telling his angry friend to calm down, he goes back to telling William about the haunted house. “Yeah, that’s right. We have a haunted house right here in our lovely little town. Believe it or not, but it is true.”

William starts laughing with disbelief. “And yet, this is the first time I’ve ever heard of anything being even remotely haunted in this town. Are you sure you are talking about this rat trap of a city?”

“And you wouldn’t have heard of this at all if you would have been minding your own business in the first place,” the Skater kid says with a mean tone in his voice.

“Yeah, you are right about that; however, your friend here doesn’t seem to mind as much as you do,” replied William in a sarcastic tone.

“Whatever.” he says while continuing to play with his stick.

The Curly head kid continues with his story. “Anyway, not many people believe in ghosts, so that’s probably why you have never heard of the story before. That is unless you watch those haunted house shows.”

William cannot help but sound sarcastic in his reply. "Sure buddy. So who are the people well ghosts that haunt this house? Or are they just people walking around at night with flashlights and sheets over their heads?" Oh wait, they could be Halloween fanatics and see this house as a means of living out their lunatic dreams of it being Halloween every day."

The Skater kid now seems to side with William in terms of believability. "This is unreal. Sounds more like a bunch of hot monkey turds than a believable story. Urban legend my ass."

The Curly head kid now seeming to be the one getting hot under the collar lets loose with his form of sarcasm. "Yeah, they are just some random people walking around the house at night with flashlights waiting to scare the crap balls out of whoever comes inside that night. Listen, it *is* as real as you and I am standing here having this conversation about this house."

"That is complete and utter beeswax in every sense of the word," says the sarcastic Skater.

"So true," as William chimes in. "Chances of this place being haunted are like one in a gazillion. Hell, I don't even know if a gazillion is even a real number."

"Believe what you want but I wouldn't go in that place if I were you. There is a curse placed on that house right along with hidden traps. Those things alone should make any one think otherwise about entering."

"So someone or something put a curse on this supposed house? Yeah right! I'll buy that for a dollar and then laugh at myself for being part of a straight up rip off scheme that some idiot cooked up in his momma's basement," says an even more sarcastic William.

With the Skater kid looking at William and laughing so hard before turning back to his friend. “You’re a funny dude! Do you honestly believe what you are saying about haunted houses? I mean seriously, the look on your face when you talk about this stuff is priceless.”

“I know that this story is true. People go in but never come out. There have been bums who went in there to find a place to sleep and have never come back out.”

William is grinning from ear to ear at this point. “How do you know that they didn’t just walk out the back door? That is possible you know.”

“Right. He must think we are completely stupid,” replied the Skater.

“That’s just it. There is no back door and the windows look completely sealed tighter than Fort Knox. Therefore, there is no way to get in or out that place except through the front door. People who go in that house need to be placed on a missing person's report. Especially if you are a bum, looking for a place to escape the elements…that would be a good spot and away from the world. Even more so, the city appears to have no plans to knock the house down or attempt to fix the place up,” said the Curly haired kid.

William is still in a sarcastic mood just adds to the unbelievable story that he is hearing right now. “So bums go in but never come out? *And* this place has a curse on the house by some unknown entity? If you say so homie.”

“What makes you think I’m lying?”

“That’s a simple answer…your mouth is moving. Plus the sound of hot garbage is spewing out with every word,” replied the

Skater.

"You are one funny cat," William says while looking at the Skater kid. "So how do you know that there is curse placed on this house in our fair and lovely city? How do you know it even exists and not just some crazed serial killer who enjoys living in that house and killing anyone who enters?"

"One, if there was a serial killer on the loose…he would either have to eat the bodies so that the smell of rotting flesh wouldn't cause suspicion or two, I'm sure he wouldn't just stop at killing bums and their little doggie companions. The curse is real. That house is who knows how damn old and yet it is not completely a run down or a collapsing building. That house definitely has something going on inside. It is no way that house should still be standing in this day and age," says the Curly haired kid.

"So explain the traps Einstein," William fires back.

"I just happened to be walking past the house and saw a flickering light on in the second floor window. There was a shadowy figure-walking pass and suddenly it disappeared as if something pulled down into the floor forcefully and then the light went out. That scared the shit out of me like no other. I hauled ass away from that place as fast as I possibly could."

"You sound like a girl," William said while laughing so hard. "So where is this house?"

"What a punk!"

"Say what you want but heed my warnings. Those who enter will never see the light of day again. Be my guest if you dare. Go to 46th and Cannon Way. 4655."

William takes a step back to look at the Curly head kid just to see his body language and to make sure that he is hearing this kid correctly. "This is unreal. This has to be the funniest load of crap I have heard in a long time. Thanks for the laughs. I would heed your warning the same way I believe junk mail about how I won a million dollars. Pushed to the side and thrown in the trash."

"If that's what you want to do then be my guest. However, if you do go and see the curse for yourself, don't say I didn't warn you."

"Thanks for that. Catch you two later my new found friends," William spots Lisa coming out the building, decides to yell, and waves in her direction. "Hey Lisa! I'm over here!"

Now Lisa is not your average student at the high school. She is not just a junior but also one of the smartest in the top two percent in the city. She is five feet five inches tall, short black Halle Berry style hair, dark brown eyes with a chocolate chip cookie complexion, all the while wearing a red shirt with short sleeves, with a pair of black shorts. To add to her being one of the smartest students in the city, she also tutors underclassmen in various subjects from math to science and one reason why William is always waiting for her after school. She is also a no nonsense type of woman who rarely does anything out of the ordinary. Her relationship with William is an odd one considering he comes off as a class clown and she is more of a bookworm.

"Hey Will. Who was that you were talking to?" she asked while watching him walk up to her.

William stops in front of Lisa and looks back at the people he just finished talking to while Lisa was coming out of the building. "I have no idea who they are. Just some guys I heard talking about some haunted house and decided to listen in to see what they were discussing," he says.

"Which was?" she asked while starting to walk home with William by her side.

"Supposedly, a cursed and booby-trapped house resides in our precious city. Personally if you ask me, the whole thing sounds like a bunch of madness but hey, what do I know?" he replied.

"Did they mention where this house was located?"

"Yes, but he also said that bums tend to go missing when they try to shack up there for the night. Plus, it's supposed to be some old run down house in midtown."

"Yeah, sure enough some like a load of hot bull to me but that's just my opinion. I didn't get to hear the whole story like you did over there. Plus this city is full of run down about to fall apart houses and other buildings," she said with a sarcastic tone.

"Yeah but the one guy was so serious about everything. He said he saw a light in the second floor window with a shadowy figure one minute; the next, the shadowy figure disappeared and the light went out instantly. So how do you explain that one?"

"Okay, he was probably just seeing things or maybe he was drinking. Not like you know them or anything like that. He or they could just be seeking attention and just wants anyone that they come across to believe their story. One never knows about kids nowadays."

"It does sound interesting though. Tell me you wouldn't want to check out a real haunted house?" he says while looking her in the eyes.

"No it doesn't. What is wrong with you? Besides there are no such thing as ghost and curses," she says adamantly while staring back at him. "You might want to look where you are going before you trip over something."

"I don't have to..."

Just as soon as she tells him to pay attention to where he is walking, William trips over a raised piece of the sidewalk. Stumbling over the sidewalk and trying to play it off as if he was dancing in the whole time. Not only was Lisa laughing at him for almost falling but also the various people that were also walking down the sidewalk. There was an outdoor flea market not even three blocks away from the school, in direct path of how the two would walk home. Therefore, many witnessed William's incident, which caused him to feel embarrassed.

"I told you to watch your step," she tells him.

"Yeah yeah," as he says while still tries to play things off despite the reaction from the crowd around him. "Anyway...," he says while checking himself to make sure there is no dirt or anything on his sneakers and continues to walk with Lisa while he is trying not to pay attention to the laughs of the crowd around him. "As I was saying. You never know for sure in this city. We do have a lot of history going on here throughout the years. Besides, the saying goes, "Where's there's a curse, there is a massive load of treasure waiting to be picked clean," he says while laughing. I swear the person who was telling me about the house just seemed a little off in the head. He just didn't seem right at all."

"You're the crazy one especially if you think there is a treasure to be had. So by my book, that makes you not so right in the head."

"Neither are you because you're with me," he says while giving Lisa a little shove on her arm.

"Whatever punk."

"Besides, if there are no such things as ghosts...care to

explain the shows that capture all the eerie voices on digital recordings."

"Sure," she says sarcastically. "Let me explain that whole ghost voice phenomenon. Hmm, let me think for a second," while rolling her thumbs over each other. "Oh yeah! They are all a bunch of phonies. There, that explains your question in the simplest form possible. Not to mention, those shows use sound effect machines and nicely timed camera glitches and cutouts with the power. Not even you can be that gullible."

"Ha ha, you are very funny Miss."

"I thought so. Now finish walking me home Mister."

The rest of the walk home is a quiet venture as they walk arm and arm down the busy streets of their little town. Passing by various shops and doing a little window-shopping, while William stands there waiting to get back home. After some more stopping and picking up ice cream along the way, William walks Lisa home and finally gets back to his house, which he is very happy to see. Upon walking into the door, Blackout comes running and jumps on William. Blackout is William's six-month-old Chow, Shepherd, and Rottweiler mix who is all black with white paws. William yells to his Mother that he is home to which she replies with, "Hi Baby. I put your food in the microwave and it still may be a little hot." William thanks his Mother and proceeds to the kitchen to get his food from the microwave before heading upstairs to his room closely followed by his favorite companion, Blackout.

William walks up the stairwell leading to the second floor, which leads to a long skinny hallway in which his room is located at the end of the narrow passage. Trying hard not to drop his food as Blackout is constantly running into William's legs while he is walking down the skinny hallway. Walking past the bathroom, which is located just feet from his room, William pushes Blackout into the bathroom with his leg hoping he will stay in there just long enough so he can open his bedroom door.

"Sit Blackout," he says while trying to turn the doorknob to his room while trying to balance his food and drink on his arm and free hand. "Now Blackout, if anything falls on the carpet, you'll have to clean it up, ok?" Blackout just looks at him with his ears pointed up with his head cocked to the side with the look of confusion. "Good boy" he says while finally getting the door to open. "Come on boy. Get on in here." With just enough light illuminating the room, William is able to see his small little table in the middle of his room in which he places his food and juice down on there before walking over to turn the light on and close the door.

"So let's see what's on television tonight Blackout. And no, we are not watching Animal Planet again" he says while turning on the television and flipping through channels. Once again, Blackout looks at him with a look of confusion while he sits in front of William wagging his tail back and forth.

William's bedroom is a typical teenage high school senior with four walls full of posters of women in bikinis and sports posters. Underneath one of the two windows, which sit right across from his bedroom door, in William's room, sits a pile of dirty clothes stacked up from the floor to the windowpane. To the left, upon entering the room, in the center of the wall is his black entertainment center, which houses a 60" LCD television equipped with a 250w surround sound system. On the opposite wall lies his king size bed with a navy blue bedding set while Blackout's dog bed lays right next to it on the floor by the headrest. In a corner along the same wall of the entertainment center stands the door to his medium sized walk in closet, which houses a ton of sneakers, designer clothing, and dozens of fitted hats from college to pro teams and a few different designers. With what little bit of the wall one can see upon entering the room that isn't covered by poster, is painted in a dark blue with a white middle breaker board and base boards with a matching shaggy floor rug coordinating with the wall paint color.

"Let's see what's on TV Blackout but I seriously doubt it will bc anything good one" while eating and looking at Blackout and handing him a piece of chicken.

He gets up, retrieves the remote for his 60" television from the entertainment center, and proceeds to hit the power button. Once the hum of the startup subsides from the television, William proceeds to flip through station after station before an eerie sound catches his attention and makes him stop in his channel flipping tracks.

"Hmm, this may be interesting. Based on a true story…is that so? I find that hard to believe," he says after hearing the narrator comment on the subject. "I guess I can watch this and see what this is all about since I didn't find anything else on. Hope you aren't scared of scary shows there Blackout," he says while looking at Blackout and petting him on the head.

William sits back and turns up the volume as the host starts to explain the story of the night.

"Good evening everyone, my name is Brock Lesenville, host of Changing Mysteries. Tonight we will cover the life and times of a pirate simply known by the name Red Point. Back in the times of pirates, in an unlikely of places known for their existence. Pirates venturing to new lands had no idea of the area or the inhabitants. Pillaging, killing the weak, and hiding their bounty of stolen treasures throughout the land that they claimed as their own. In a time where piracy was a way of life and was lived by the code of honor amongst thieves, one city of little known origin was home to a powerful and feared pirate simply known as Red Point. Red Point was born of humble beginnings on a little island southeast of The United States. So small was this island, that it was barely visible on a map. His parents were both farmers who often struggled to make ends meet for his family. Around his twelfth birthday, ravenous thugs ransacked their farm and burned it to the ground murdering Red Point's mother and father. Red Point was then an orphan thrust into the peasant street life as a beggar and had to resort to being a thief to survive. It was then, that pirates unofficially adopted him. Lead by Captain Peter "The Viking" Blatz, Red Point was raised to be a pirate in every since of the word. By the time he was seventeen, Red Point plundered, pillaged, and murdered his way to being the most feared pirate of all time. Red Point was hung at the age of 25 for his crimes against the helpless people whom he terrorized during his reign…it is said to believe that he hid what could be worth $35 million dollars by today's standards in a now highly populated city of Starside, Pennsylvania. Before the lever was pulled, he vowed to reclaim all that was his in 500 years or if his treasures were ever disturbed by anyone but him. This is all just a story passed down from generation to generation but no one has ever located any trace of the treasure or the area in which he stashed his possessions. Stay tuned for…"

"Makes me wonder if this was what that kid from school was talking about earlier," he says while turning off the television. "Bunch of craziness but how nice would it be to find that money? Imma take my ass to bed. Hate having to get up early. Blackout, get up and turn the light off, why don't you?" Blackout lifts his head up off his bed with it cocked to the side and gives a look of "No," to William, which causes him to say, "Silly dog," as he slowly has to get up out of bed and turns the light off himself before falling asleep in a matter of minutes upon returning to his bed.

Chapter Two

The Setup

It has been two weeks now since William first learned of the haunted house in the city in which he calls home. Since that eventful conversation after school while waiting to walk Lisa home, William has been unable to think about anything else except to find this mysterious house. Not once has he ever considered this a joke or a hoax, he then proceeds to let his friends in on the tidbit of information that he discovered over the last couple of weeks.

William has been doing a lot of thinking about whether or not to unveil this information to his friends and not wanting them to think he is a little loony in the head or needing a padded room for himself. After school one day, he meets with Marcus to discuss plans for the weekend and to tell him of his discovery and conversation with the other two kids after school that one day two weeks ago. As Marcus and himself stand on the corner of 56th and Vineyard leaning on the high chain link fence that surrounds the outside of the school before going their separate ways home.

"Damn it feels good to be out of this bullshit ass school for the day," William says while looking down at his watch. "This has been one of the longest days ever and all I want to do is go home and relax."

"I feel you on that one homie. What is up with Mr. Reckles and all this homework lately? I was about to cuss him out when he finished assigning us this madness," replied Marcus. "I can't believe he did this to us…again."

Marcus is your typical quiet person until you get to know

him. He's about five feet ten inches tall, a little on the slim side with a close cut with trimmed sideburns and goatee. He's the quiet yet sneaky type and has no problem walking right up on you and scaring whoever he targets. He has a good heart and always there to help his friends in need. Dressed wearing his usual colors of a navy blue and white shirt that stops just below his belt line with navy blue shorts, white socks, and some navy blue and white sneakers, all topped off with a navy blue Kaged Wun fitted hat.

"I know M. Ten chapters to read plus answer the stupid questions at the end of each chapter. That cat lucky it's Friday and we won't have to see him for another two days." Suddenly William hears his name being called, only to turn and notices a car full of young women screaming for his attention. "Hey ladies, give me a call this weekend and let me know what's going down." He waves to them as they go speeding off on a green light then turns to Marcus. "I will definitely need my rest after dealing with them this weekend."

"Yeah, I don't see how that's going to happen considering you're with Lisa. So what's really going on this weekend playboy?"

"Really Marcus? Why you gotta clown a brotha man like that? Won't even let me fantasize. Anyway, you might be a little scared after what I'm about to tell you."

"Yeah right," says Marcus while brushing off his scared comment. "Can't be no worse than the time you jumped because of a cat coming out of the bushes."

"Ha ha, real funny smartass. Do you want to hear the plan or not?"

"Go for it."

"Ok. Now this may sound a little crazy at first but it was on one of those haunted specials. Supposedly and I said supposedly now. There is a house here in our fair city that is haunted *AND* has a hidden treasure inside somewhere."

"You're kidding me right," says Marcus while trying hard not to laugh hysterically in William's face. "Do you really think a show is a reliable source of information?"

"Good enough for me to believe that it's real enough to do a documentary on something that could have happened in our very own city. Plus they showed what the area looked like before and they showed how the place would look now."

"Seriously Will. You really believe it's a real haunted house homie?"

"Yes."

"That's some carnival urban legend type shit right there though."

"So you down or what Marcus? Or are you just going to punk out on me"

"Seriously Will? When was the last time you saw me punk out? I'm not losing no challenge to you or any of your so-called stories. So who else is coming with us?"

"Lisa and Janet if they don't get all scared and decide to stay at home and do their hair," William says while laughing a little bit. "But hey, who knows when it comes to those two."

"I'm sure if Janet goes then Lisa will go too. Those two are like two peas in a pod...usually. So what makes you think this story is true just based off of what you saw on some late night show?"

"Well, I'm just going off of what they said plus it's from a reliable network who deals in this type of stuff."

Marcus is just looking at William with a raised left eyebrow and a questionable look on his face. "You're kidding me right? It's no way a reliable; throws up air quotes with his hands, network even exist in this world. Let alone one that claims to have information on a haunted house in our hometown and be real."

"Yeah well, so the script says anyway."

Walking under the tree to get some Shade. "Are you bullshitting me on this Will? Something doesn't sound about right with this story. Just from my point of view."

"You know that's not my style homie. I wouldn't do that to you."

"So if this is true, why hasn't anyone looked for this place before?"

"Hell if I know Marcus. I guess they didn't believe it was true either. Maybe it was good for network television at the time. Who knows?"

"True. You know I'm down. Seeing this for myself would make me a believer but until then, you know I'm going to be skeptical. So when are we going?"

"Tomorrow and I'll have Janet and Lisa meet us. Then I'll call you once I talk to Lisa and give you the time."

"Cool…where's the meet up?

"I'll call you after I talk to Lisa. You call Janet after I call you and see if she'll go or not. I'm sure she will though. She's in to this kind of stuff. By the time we talk, I can definitely tell you where and when and we'll all just meet up then. All I'm going to say is you better not be a no show or you're getting clowned for life with a giant billboard on the highway."

"You're a funny dude," Marcus says while leaning away from the tree and brushing off the back of his pants. "You better worry about your girl not standing you up on this little adventure. She might be the one who is a no show."

"We'll see who gets clowned tomorrow," Will replies while walking up to give daps to Marcus before going on his way home to call Lisa. "Better hope Janet shows up. Don't want you to be the third wheel with no one to talk to."

"You got jokes. Holla when you get word on tomorrow. I'm out. One advantage of living close to school. I don't have far to walk in this hot sun."

"And somehow you still manage to be late for class."

"What can you say, it's an acquired skill. Don't hate the player homie.'

"Later Marcus."

The two go their separate ways home in the warm afternoon. While William is on his way home, he is contemplating on how to explain the plan to Lisa and what's going to happen. As he is thinking it over in his head, the idea just sounds crazier and crazier. However, he still thinks this is a real event and cannot wait to see this plan out to the end. Walking down the congested blocks of North Vineyard Ave, there seems to be block parties for miles going on. Paying the parties no mind, he continues on his way home when a man suddenly approaches him and hands him a flier.

"Excuse me sir. Will you take this flyer?" the slightly older man says while handing a flier to William as he walks by.

"What's this flyer for?" William asked as he stops to accept the flyer.

"To open your mind and to accept reality as things are."

The man appears to be in his late fifties with a brown cane in his left hand. Standing no taller than five foot four inches tall, with a grayish-black hair with a beard to match, a long nose and chiseled chin and pointy ears. His clothing was not of that of a person attending a block party, seeing as he is dressed in worn down black business type suit with a white button down shirt.

As William is holding the flyer in his hand, he gets an eerie feeling all over his body. "This is a little weird. Open my mind to what reality exactly?"

"One you will see very shortly."

"Oh kay now. Well, I'll be seeing you around." as William starts walking away while looking down at the flyer. "This is some freaky "Twilight Zone" shit." As he looks down to continue reading the blue flyer with white letters. The paper begins to feel warm in his hand as if it was just printed. He notices that his fingerprints are appearing on the paper as he continues reading.

He stops in his tracks and turns around to see if the man that gave him the flyer is still around but to no avail. "This is freaky. How can he be there one minute and gone the next. Open my mind. Who puts something like that on a flyer and gives them out to people?" As he is holding the paper, it begins to get hotter.

William instinctively drops the paper as he watches it burn to ash and disintegrates before hitting the ground. With shock and amazement as to what he just witnessed, William is flushed with his heartbeat racing and a sense of anxiety rushes over him. After standing there for what seems like five minutes to him after seeing what just happens, William takes off running to his house.

With William finally arriving home after his crazy encounter with a random stranger on the street and sweating up a storm in the process. He makes it to his room where he sees Blackout waiting for him at his room door. “Hey boy. How are you?” William asked Blackout who just looks at him with his head cocked to the side and his ears are pointing up.

William then proceeds to sit in front of his fan to cool off after running home. “Can’t wait to tell Marcus about this craziness. Blackout, I should have taken you with me on that one. It’s just to bad you couldn’t come with me to school today. Could have used you after dealing with that guy.” Blackout just barks and starting wagging his tail excitingly.

After several minutes of sitting under the fan to cool off, William gets up and changes out of his school uniform and into something more relaxing.

Still a little freaked out about what happened earlier, William reaches for his cellphone to call Lisa to fill her in on today’s events and to inform her of the meet up tomorrow.

“She better answer her phone.” he says while dialing Lisa’s number while lying on his bed.

After about four rings, Lisa finally answer her phone. “Hello.”

“Hey baby. What’s going on tonight?”

“Who’s this?” she says in a questionable tone.

“If you don’t know then I sure as hell won’t be telling you.” sounding kind of upset but also in a joking manner.

Just to mess with William and send him over the edge, Lisa stops and thinks for a second. “Hmm…Is it William? How are you?”

“Real funny Miss. After a greeting like that one. You should be telling me what’s going on. All good though, I hold no grudges against you smartass. I called because it’s something I have to talk to you about.”

“Which would be what?” she asked sounding intrigued.

“How would you like to go to a haunted house?”

Lisa goes eerily quiet over there prompting William to ask if she was still there.

She calmly asks, “What in the hell have you been smoking over there?”

“Nothing.”

“Drinking? Or is whatever you’re on even legal?”

William can’t help but laugh at Lisa thinking it’s something wrong with him for asking such a question. “No and it’s legal. Trust me on this one. Marcus and I are going to check it out and wanted to know if you and Janet would join us.”

“When?”

“Tomorrow. What time? I don’t know. I’ll have to get back to you on that one.”

“Well, tomorrow I have to babysit and I’m sure as hell won’t be bringing those kids with me.”

“So you’re down?”

“Sure. Any time after four is good with me,” she says while trying not to sound so creeped out by the offer.

“Cool. I’ll call you back in a few minutes and let you know.”

“Just don’t forget to call me back.”

“I won’t,” he says sounding so reassuring. “Bye lady.”

“Bye Mister.”

“Wait a minute,” William says trying to catch Lisa before she hangs up. “I got something else to tell you.”

The line is silent for a second before Lisa responds, “What? Did you forget something?”

“You will not believe the craziness that happened on my way home after chilling with Marcus after school.”

“Is that so? Try me.”

“Ok,” he says while taking a deep breath. “It was this old man standing on the block while I was walking home. Ok, no big deal. So then he gives me this flyer that only said, “To open your mind and to accept reality as things are.”

“What?” she says sounding surprised.

“That’s not the crazy part,” he calmly says. “The paper started burning in my hand.”

“Stop lying!”

“No lies baby girl. The paper started getting hot and eventually caught fire. I looked for the man but he was gone. I don’t know where he went. It was like he vanished into thin air.”

Now Lisa is sounding more skeptical about what she just heard. “So the paper caught fire and the guy just disappeared?”

“Yes.”

“You sure this wasn’t a dream for you?” Lisa asked in a skeptical tone.

“Uh…yeah” William says as he starting to sound upset about Lisa not believing his story.

“Oh calm down ya big baby. If you said it happened then I believe you. Would be kind of hard to make up something like this out the blue.”

“Whatever you say,” wanting to hang up on her but he pauses. “I will talk to you tomorrow. I have to call Marcus.”

“Ok, don’t be mad baby.”

“Not mad at all,” he says trying to sound convincing.

“Bye.”

“Talk to you in a bit Lisa.”

The two hang up as William starts searching for Marcus’s number so he can give him a call on the details about the meet up. “I have no idea what I did with his number,” as he searches on his desk and flipping through papers and inside of his notebooks. “Uhhhhh,” sounding upset that he can’t find the phone number. “Will definitely save this number in my phone this time when I find it.”

Looking at Blackout who is just staring at William while he searches for Marcus’s number. “Don’t just look at me like that Blackout. Help a brotha look for this number.” Flipping through the last notebook that was on the bottom of a stack of papers and finally finding the number written in the back of the book. "About damn time," he says with a sigh of relief.

As William finishes dialing Marcus's number, he makes sure to save it in his cellphone as a new contact. "This fool better answer his phone. Hate talking to stupid voicemails."

The phone rings almost four times before Marcus picks up the phone. "What's going on sucka?" Marcus says when he picks up the phone.

"How'd you know it's me fool?"

"Really Will? It's called caller id and even before I saw the number, I have ringtones for every one of my contacts. Not that hard to figure out."

"Yeah whatever fool!" William says laughing. "So here's the scoop. Lisa is down to go but she has to babysit before we meet up."

"Ok cool," Marcus says while nodding his head. "Then I'll call Janet once we get off the phone and see if she's not a chicken."

"Lisa did think I was high or drunk when I told her about the whole idea at first," William says sarcastically.

"Can you blame her though?"

"So plan is that once she is done babysitting duties, we can swing by and pick her up and head on over and get Janet."

"Sounds like a plan homie. Or maybe she can just meet us somewhere," Marcus says in a questionable tone.

"That might be easier to do," William says while spinning around in his desk chair, "but you have to call Janet because I don't have her number."

"Not a problem. I'll call you back after I talk to her and see if she's down to ride."

"Cool homie."

"Peace dawg."

"Be easy," William says while in the process of hanging up the phone.

Jumping over to Marcus's house while he is preparing to call Janet to see if she is going to go to the haunted house or will she punk out. He is up in his room with the music blasting some old school hip-hop with his room decorated in basketball posters, the typical high school senior with dreams of making it big one day and owning his own mansion.

While Marcus is laying on his bed looking at his phone so he can call Janet about the plans, he's flipping through his phone to get to her number. "This ought to be an interesting conversation," he says while hitting the call button next to her name. "I know she'll go…"

Janet's phone rings once before she answers, "Speak and this better be important," she says in a sarcastic creole accent.

As Marcus begins to speak, he decides to change his voice to sound like a bill collector. "Hi. May I speak to Janet Den-May please?"

"Who?" she replies.

"Janet Deen-May."

"For one, it's Janet DeMay and two, she's not here."

Still using his bill collector voice, "Ok, can you have her call Marcus at…"

Janet interrupts him as soon as she hears Marcus, "You are such a punk. What's going on?"

Marcus just laughs before answering, "Just chilling."

"So what are you up to?

Janet is a character within herself of characters. She's five foot eight inches with the body of a model. She's a captain on the basketball team as she's the team's starting shooting guard. The life of the party when things get dull as she enjoys being the wild and crazy one. Long straight black hair that is a little past her shoulders which she likes to wear in a ponytail, she's light skinned with a few freckles around her nose and cheek area. Wearing basic loungewear of shorts and a t-shirt while talking to Marcus.

"Calling to see what you've been doing and what if you're down to ride out?"

"Well," she pauses for a second, "some fool keeps on calling here reciting poetry in my ear and what not. I think it was LeRoy again."

"That sounds like something he would do. I'll remember that when I ask you to listen to one of my poems next time."

"No, it's nothing like that" she says in a hurry. "I just know that you wouldn't call unless something was going on."

"True but while I don't completely agree with that statement at all, I did call for a reason."

"Well, what is it? I'm in the middle of my workout."

"Well isn't he mad that you're on the phone," he says

sarcastically while trying not to laugh.

"Wha…?" she replies in a questionable tone.

"Nothing. Do you want to go to a haunted house?"

"A haunted house? Is that all. Why didn't you just say so in the first.."

Before she could finish her sentence, Marcus cuts her off. "It's a real haunted house. Not an amusement park theme adventure."

Janet sounds a little surprised by that statement. "Oh really now?"

"Yes. So you down to ride or chicken out?"

"Yeah, I guess I will go. Seriously doubt it's really haunted."

"I guess we will see," he says back to her. "When I talk to Will again, I'll call you back and let you know where we're meeting."

"Ok," Janet says in a tone of doubt over this haunted house.

"Now get back to your workout Ghetto Fonda."

"Real funny Marcus. Just make sure you call me back."

"Will do my lady."

"Bye Marcus."

"Later J."

Just as Marcus is hanging up with Janet, he receives a weird text message from an unknown blocked number. Since he has his phone set up so he can see the first couple lines of the text before opening the message, he was able to see that the message read, “Don’t Go!” Thinking nothing of the message he then goes and deletes it from his inbox. The message comes through again as if the sender knew the message was deleted. “Don’t Go!” appears again in his inbox from an unknown blocked number.

“What in the hell?” he says while looking strangely at his phone. “Who the hell would be sending me “Don’t Go!” messages to my phone and how’d whoever get my number?”

Once again he deletes the message from his phone and just as fast as it was deleted, it reappears in his inbox. Raising his eyebrows in a questionable manner, he starts contemplating on whether to just open the message and send a replay. Slowly starting to pace back and forth between his desk and his bed, he goes back to his inbox with his finger hovering over the unknown number’s message.

“Ok, this is a little creepy. Why am I getting this message?” he says as he continues to pace back and forth.

The same message comes through again and then three seconds later it happens again. After about fifteen seconds, the message has flooded his inbox with over forty messages all saying, “Don’t Go!” before he throws his phone on the bed and jumping back.

“This is getting out of hand,” he thinks to himself while being slightly scared. Suddenly his phone starts going crazy with text notifications non-stop for over a minute then just stops for no apparent reason. When he walks over to his bed and checks his inbox, there are 78 unread text messages from the same unknown restricted number all saying, “Don’t Go!”

“Screw this. Let me call Lisa because this is some

craziness. No one is going to believe this story."

"Ok, let me collect myself. Can't call Lisa sounding all shook," he thinks to himself while hitting the call button on Lisa's number.

Lisa's phone rings three times before she answers her phone while sounding like she ran up the steps to answer the call.

"Hello?"

"What's going on babygirl?"

"And you are?"

"Well finish this line," he says with a smirk on his face.

"Ok."

"Who's your-"

Lisa answers the question in a surprising tone. "Daddy?"

"I knew I'd get you to say that one day," he says while laughing hard.

"Shut up smartass."

"No can do lady."

"So what's going on Marcus?" she says while jumping on her bed and stretching out.

"When do you get off from the babysitting job tomorrow?"

"About 4:30ish or so."

"Cool. We were just going to meet up somewhere and just wait until you got done."

"Where?" she asks.

"Didn't really pick a spot but how about we meet on the corner 41st and Spellrod Blvd."

Lisa just starts thinking of all places why he would pick that place to meet up. Seeing as though it used to be an old music store turned nostalgic arcade.

"Ok, not a problem. I know where that is. You think this place is actually haunted? Will seems to think this place is real."

Marcus begins laughing just a little bit to himself.

"Hell. Anything is possible in this screwed up world."

"So what's the catch?" she asks.

Marcus pauses for a second trying to decide whether she is joking while walking around his room with the phone to his ear.

"No catch. Just going along to see how real this story really is. Plus Will seems to think it's legit and from a reliable source. So who knows for sure."

"Reliable," she says starting to laugh. "I was there when he was getting this reliable news. It came from some skater kids."

"I guess we shall see tomorrow."

"Yeah, let's hope we don't end up on the news as four dead teenagers found buried under rumble after the building collapses on us."

"We'll be fine. Stop thinking the worse. It's probably just another old house that creeks when the wind blows to hard. Anyway, be there tomorrow or be clowned."

"Real funny Mister. I'll see you tomorrow."

"See you then Lisa."

"Bye Marcus."

As Marcus is hanging up with Lisa, he sits on the edge of his bed debating whether he should have told Lisa about the crazy text messages. He then puts down his phone knowing that he has to call Janet and William back in order to tell them he talked to Lisa about tomorrow's meet up time and place. As he takes a deep breath and falls back onto his bed, he quickly jumps out of shock as his phone suddenly goes off. Marcus's heart starts racing while he reaches for his phone.

Reaching for his phone not knowing what to expect, he sees it's a text from Janet.

"In case you forgot, you better call me back"

Taking a deep breath. "So happy that was her and not that unknown number," he says while feeling his heart racing through his chest. "That's a relief."

Instead of calling Janet and William back, Marcus just decides to send them a text about tomorrow and kills two birds with one stone. Composing a group message for the two of them.

"Talked to Lisa and she'll meet us tomorrow after babysitting at 41st and Spellrod Blvd."

Almost instantly they both text back, “Ok.” As if they were synchronized automated response messages for being out of work, the message come back to Marcus in a matter of seconds apart from each other.

Having to text William back about getting some information on this so called haunted house so he can do his own research before tomorrow’s meetup. Texting William just to get basic information about this house and a little background information if he knew any.

“William, hit me back and send me some information about this haunted house or whatever you know.”

William sends Marcus the information he heard from the television show that he watched before telling him about the haunted house and wanting to check it out. At first he couldn’t remember the name of the pirate in question before sending three more additional texts reconfirming the correct name and his backstory. With this newly acquired information, Marcus hops out of bed and onto the computer to see if he can find any information about a pirate named Red Point and information about a haunted house associated with that name.

On the other side of the friendship circle…Janet and Lisa are on the phone talking about the haunted house conspiracy and whether it’s real. Having a good time joking about the whole situation and potential events of tomorrow.

“So which of the two idiots called you about tomorrow?” Lisa asks Janet while trying her hardest not to laugh about the question.

"Marcus. Plus he sent me a text before we got on the phone."

"Sounds like a bunch of idiocy to me but I told Marcus I'd be there tomorrow after I finished babysitting," says Lisa.

"A haunted house in our city and yet there are no stories about anything going on. Let along an urban legend about the place."

"Well J. Things are a little odd about this city. People are crazy all over. Look who set this whole thing up and we both know Will is off his rocker."

"Well, he *is* your boyfriend Lisa," Janet says while trying not to laugh to hard. "But seriously though, never know what could happen dealing with his crazy ass." Walking down her steps and heading towards the kitchen. "I'll be there with those knuckleheads too. So we can call it a day with the homies."

"True. I really don't want to go to work but I need that money. Plus you can see Marcus tomorrow. You know you feeling him. Stop playing before he ends up with someone else."

"Real funny girl. That's just my friend."

"Says the woman who is putting up a major wall on everyone but him," Lisa says in a sarcastic tone.

"Whatever Lisa. I'll see you tomorrow around 4:30."

"Bye Janet."

"Bye Lisa."

"Hold on J," Lisa says trying to catch Janet before she hangs up but she is a second to late. "Oh well, I'll see her tomorrow."

Chapter Three

The Meet Up

On a nice warm Saturday afternoon, the whole gang meets up at 41st and Spellrod Blvd's busy street in front of the Mad Gamer Arcade around 4:35pm. A place where the whole crew knows since it has been on Spellrod Blvd for the last six years and have spent countless hours and a bucket load of quarters. The entrance of the arcade looks like a drawbridge with a castle exterior surrounding the entrance. Two snipers perches, one on each side of the door sit atop the building. Painted with a dragon scaling the right side of the wall of the building and a knight on the other.

The only one missing from the entertaining busy streets and warm gathering is Lisa. Who; per the usual, is always running late. The streets, packed with kids are running in and out of the Mad Gamer, people running in and out of the local shops and street vendors are yelling to get the attention of passersby. Traffic is crazy as usual for a Saturday afternoon with people darting in and out of traffic causing horns to fill the air and screams of name-calling from the angry drivers.

Janet, Marcus and William are just standing around talking to each other while waiting on Lisa to show. All are wearing shorts and tees with their own flash of style and combination of different graphics.

"Yo William! Where ya girl at homie?" Marcus asked.

"Like I know. I am not her personal keeper. I know she needs to hurry up because this bag is getting heavy," William replies.

"What in the hell is in that thing?" Janet asked in a surprising tone.

"Stuff," he replies.

"Sure, call it what you want Will," Janet says sarcastically.

Looking in Janet's direction. "Have you heard from Lisa?" Marcus asked.

"Not at all."

"I know she needs to hurry her little ass up. I'll go down the block to see if I can see her coming," Marcus says while flexing the rim on his hat to better block out the sun.

"I'll come get you personally," Janet says in a sexy voice with her hands on her hips.

"Yeah! Go get'er homie!" William says excitingly.

"You know it's not like that Will," Janet responds while watching Marcus take off walking down the block laughing and waving back to them.

Marcus starts walking down the block towards the train station trying to see if Lisa is walking up the block while William holds his hand over his head to shade his face from the bright sun. Janet runs into a clothing store two doors down from the Mad Gamer Arcade with the hopes of buying a new outfit for her next date night.

As soon as she is reaching for the handle of the clothing store, Marcus is texting Janet that he sees Lisa coming up the street.

"Aye Janet! Don't even go in there!"

Janet feels her phone vibrate in her pocket and proceeds to check her messages.

"Aww man, I wanted to run in this store," Janet says in a sad tone while looking in the window at a red skirt and jacket combination that was dressed on a mannequin with a sale tag on the left jacket pocket. "One day you will be mines," she says while walking back down to the Mad Gamer to join the group.

Just as Lisa and Marcus make it back to the Mad Gamer Arcade, Janet is no more than a few steps away from the group. Not even ten minutes have passed before everyone is standing in front of the arcade wondering what happened to Lisa and why she is so late.

"Look who decides to join us," William says sarcastically while leaning in to hug Lisa.

"It's been a long day and it got weirder on the way here," Lisa responds while hugging everyone in the group. "It was just crazy."

"What happened?" Janet asks with concern in her voice.

"Ok, let me start from the beginning."

Everyone is just looking at Lisa as she begins to tell her story while they are walking towards one of the local eateries on the block.

Just one hour ago, Lisa was preparing to leave her babysitting job in order to meet up with everyone else on 41st and

Spellrod Blvd. Not having any idea what would be waiting for her once she started her journey uptown.

As a way to make a little extra money, Lisa babysits a five-year-old boy and a four-year-old little girl while their mother works morning shift at a local hospital. Things started out like any other Saturday on the job. The kids gave Lisa a run for her money today as they were running amok in the living room and throwing couch cushions at each other ten minutes before lunchtime. As Lisa is making lunch while trying to keep an eye on the situation, she prepares peanut butter and jelly sandwiches and cannot wait until it's naptime. Cutting up the sandwiches and putting them on the kid's plate along with pouring milk into a glass for each of them.

"Come and eat Mike and Courtney," she says while placing everything on the table in front of where the kids will seat.

The two come running into the kitchen like speed racers and jump into their seats to eat lunch. Mike is the first to reach his seat while Courtney is a couple of seconds behind him. With both of them at the kitchen table, Lisa sits at the island in the middle of the massive kitchen, in which high priced wooden cabinets surround the area. Stainless steel appliances everywhere from the refrigerator to the double bake stove and dishwasher. There is even a trash compacter built into the middle of the island in which Lisa is sitting.

Lisa works for a very well to do doctor. As she looks up from her paperwork in the direction of the kids, she sees Mike waving to her.

She waves back to him before asking if he is ok and if he needs anything. He just smile back at her and says, "Thank you Miss Lisa for lunch," before continuing to drink the rest of his milk.

"You're welcome Mike," she says back before going back to filling out her paperwork.

A few minutes later, Mike jumps out of his seat and runs over the Lisa with plate in hand.

"I'm all finished Miss Lisa," he says while handing her his plate.

"Where's your cup?"

"I'll go get it," he says while running back to the table.

"Careful Mike."

In a matter of seconds, Mike returns with cup in hand. "Here is my cup," he says while handing over his cup.

"Thank you Mike. Now what time is it?"

"Naptime Miss Lisa," he replies.

"That's right. Go get ready and I'll be in the living room in a second," she says before asking Courtney if she's ok.

Courtney just nods her head and continues to eat the last bit of her sandwich.

Lisa looks at her watch and just thinks to herself that she hopes she can meet up with the crew on time. "I'm going to be cutting it close."

Out the corner of her eye, Lisa see Courtney with plate and cup in hand ready to give them to her. "Thank you Courtney."

Courtney just smiles and runs into the living room to lay down for her nap. With Lisa right behind her to double check on the kids before they fall asleep and make sure they are comfortable. Upon entering the living room, Lisa spots Mike on the couch already sleep and Courtney getting comfortable in front of the fireplace while laying on her blanket and using a couch cushion as a pillow.

"Sleep well Courtney. See you when you wake up."

Courtney just smiles back before closing her eyes.

In what seemed like minutes, Mike and Courtney's Mom is walking into the house three hours later. She sees that the kids are still sleeping and tries to be quiet while making her way over to Lisa who is studying in the kitchen.

Whispering so she doesn't wake the kids. "How'd things go today Lisa?" she asked.

"Things were good Mrs. Jefferson. The usual run around, eat, and pass out routine," she replies.

"Thank you so much for today. I can always count on you," Mrs. Jefferson says while going in her wallet to give Lisa her payment.

Mrs. Jefferson hands Lisa one hundred and fifty dollars.

Taking the money and thinking it's too much. "I think you gave me to much," she says to Mrs. Jefferson.

"No I didn't. It's the right amount," she says. "You deserve a little something extra for doing such a good job with these two wild children."

"T-Thank you," Lisa says sounding surprised by the raise. "I appreciate this."

"You're welcome but you are really appreciated and the

kids adore you so much."

Lisa starts packing up her books and papers in order to leave to meet the crew. "I adore those little monsters too," Lisa replies.

As Lisa puts the last book into her bag and zips everything up, the kids start waking up from their nap. Mike is the first one up and running to his mother.

"Mommy!" Mike says all excited running with arms wide open towards her.

Before Mrs. Jefferson even realizes, Courtney is hugging her leg with a big smile on her face.

"Mommy is home. How are my babies?"

"Good," says Mike.

"Did you behave for Miss Lisa?"

The two just nod their heads.

"Miss Lisa is getting ready to leave. You want to say goodbye?"

The two run over to Lisa and give her a hug as she hugs them back.

"I'll see you two real soon. Be good for your Mommy or I am going to come back and tickle you."

Courtney hugs Lisa and smiles before running off into the living room with Mike right behind her.

"Thanks again for everything Lisa. You're a life saver."

"Anytime Mrs. Jefferson," she says while heading to the

door.

With Mrs. Jefferson right behind her, they both walk to the door.

Opening the door and looking back at Mrs. Jefferson, "I will see you next Saturday."

"Not a problem. You actually don't have to come next week but I'll pay you for that day anyway. I'm taking the kids to see their grandparents in Vale City," explains Mrs. Jefferson.

In total shock by what she just heard, Lisa has no idea how to respond to this situation. "Um…thank you," she says in complete shock while walking out the door.

"Don't mention it. Have a good day Lisa," she says while waving goodbye to Lisa who is halfway down the walkway.

Still in a euphoric state after receiving a bonus from Mrs. Jefferson and waving goodbye to her, Lisa heads off to catch the train in order to meet her friends at the arcade while plugging one of her earbuds into her left ear. It is a nice day out with a good breeze in the suburbs of Shell Valley West.

An area of the city where you would have to make at least one hundred thousand a year just to think about buying a house in this area of town. Streets are so clean that even the ripped up pieces of floating paper in the wind land in recycling bins that line the streets of this quiet neighborhood. Every house has a nicely manicured lawn and tall stylish hedges line a majority of the properties along this street. Producing magazine quality work, the landscaper's service must cost a pretty penny. Several homes in Lisa's path have three and even four car garages.

As Lisa is walking down the long block that seems to go on forever, something catches her attention out the corner of her left eye. She suddenly stops next to a high brick wall with a six foot high metal black pillar fence with spade points that adorn the tops of each post. As she looks through the metal fencing, she spots what caught her attention. A hedge. Not just any hedge but one that is cut into a ten foot tall T-Rex that sits in the middle of a circular driveway surrounded by various colored flowers which sits fifty or sixty yards from the wall.

"Now that takes some skill," she thinks to herself. Wondering just how much time and effort went into designing and cutting the hedge. She looks to the right of that fantastic design to see another in the shape of what appears to be a raptor, surrounded also by brightly colored flowers.

"This person must really like dinosaurs and flowers," she says peering through the bars of the fence.

Walking up the street along the fence towards the train station, tall hedges are starting to line up along the fence blocking the view to the property. What little she can see of the remaining property, there are a few more hedges designed in the shape of dinosaurs. Getting to the corner of the property and the street, she notices something rustling in the bushes by the fence. Thinking nothing of the noise, she proceeds to walk away from the fence when the rustling gets louder causing her to look back towards the fence.

With a questionable look on her face, she stops and looks towards the fence. Starting to get an eerier feeling run down her body, when suddenly a black shadow crashes loudly into the metal fence causing a loud clanging sound. Lisa jumps back swiftly in fear so fast that she hits a mailbox sitting on the corner of the block.

Trying to stop her heart from racing by taking deep breaths,

Lisa notices a pain on the lower left side of her back from where she hit the mailbox.

Reaching back across the front of her body with her right hand and rubbing the spot near the middle of her ribcage. “Hopefully that doesn’t leave a mark,” she says while gently touching the area. “This is starting to turn into the day from hell. And what the hell hit the fence like that?”

Looking to see if anyone else in the area heard the loud noise. There is no one in the area as if the streets suddenly became a ghost town. Taking a second to gather herself, she looks up at the fence to see that the bars are bent outwards towards the street.

“What in the…” she says before being interrupted by a man asking if she is ok.

“Are you ok Miss?” the stranger asks of Lisa.

“Um…yes, t-thank you for asking,” she replies looking confused. “Where did you come from? The streets were just empty.”

“The bus stop across the street behind you. This is a very busy section of the city.”

“B-But, the streets were just deserted. What happened?” she says while looking at the man and then looking at the fence. “The fence. Look at the fence.”

The man looks at the fence and then looks back at Lisa who is now leaning on the mailbox.

“What am I looking at young lady?” he asks Lisa.

“The rods are bent outward towards the street,” she says pointing in the direction of the fence before looking in that direction.

The man looks at Lisa as if she is going insane or has been drinking. “The fence is fine. There is nothing wrong with the structure. Did you hit your head to hard?”

“No, I am ok. Thank you. I have to get going.”

Lisa still looking surprised about the fence continues walking on her way to the train station. As she looks back at the fence, she can see that the fence is slightly bent outward versus how it was originally before the man came over to check on her.

“I know I’m not crazy. What is going on here?” she asks herself while walking towards the train station. The rest of the way to the station, Lisa listens to her music while still being a little shaken by what happened with the fence.

After arriving to the underground train station and Lisa swipes her school badge at a turnstile, she stands at the platform waiting for her train.

“I am going to be so late,” she says to herself while looking at her watching showing 4:15pm. “What a day, what a day. Got a bonus and easy money for next week and then I have a weird episode with a fence. This is not how…”

Suddenly a man walks up to Lisa while pulling a small black suitcase on wheels behind him. He looks homely, a thin long red dirty and oil stained jacket, kind of a scruffy beard, with black sneakers and thin black track pants and a close black haircut.

“Excuse me Miss. You appear to be having a bad day. Might I interest you in some of my relaxation oils?” he says while standing next to Lisa with a smile on his face.

“No thank you,” she replies while looking at her watch

again.

"Have on one the house. I insist. No charge," he says while reaching into his bag while pulling out a four-ounce bottle. "This is Beaded Moons, one of my top sellers and I'll give it to you for free.

"Thank you but I can't take anything from you."

"I insist. I don't do this for just anyone. You strike me as a nice young lady who appears to be highly stressed out. Now what you do is dab a little drop on the wrist, rub them together, and take a smell of the aroma. The aroma will release a pleasant smell that will almost instantly cause a calming effect to the senses."

Lisa leans over to look down the track line to see the train is soon to arrive at the station.

"About time," she says.

"So will you take this gift? I insist," he asks her again.

"Sure," she says while looking at the man. "If this is as good as you say, I will come back and buy a few bottles from you."

"Thank you so much," he says while handing Lisa the four-ounce bottle.

The train arrives at the platform and the doors open to only a few people getting off the train. As Lisa is stepping onto the train, she turns to thank the man for the gift.

"Thank you very much."

"You're welcome young lady. May you have a good day," he says while watching the doors close to the train.

As Lisa goes to look for a seat, she glances back to see that the man is no longer on the platform.

"This has truly been a weird day," she says while grabbing one of the poles that connect to the ceiling of the train car by the seat. "This place is packed."

Without warning, there is an announcement over the intercom as the train starts to come to a crawl and then to a complete stop between the 18th Street Station and 33rd Street Station.

"Attention riders. Sorry for the disruption of service but there has been a malfunction on the track just before the 33rd Street Station. Within ten to fifteen minutes, the problem will be fixed and we will be arriving at your destination shortly. Thank you again for riding with Public Trailways Transportation Services," says the Conductor over the intercom.

The entire train lets off a disgruntled moan as soon as the announcement is finished.

"This is some bullshit!" a man shouts that is standing next to Lisa. As well as an outburst from a woman standing to the right of Lisa, "I have kids in daycare. This stupid company is getting my late charges billed to them!"

The entire train car erupts into laughter after hearing these two shouting.

Lisa grabs her phone out of her purse in an attempt to call one of her friends. "Damn! No service," she says while looking at her phone. "Can this day get any better?"

"Couldn't agree with you more," another woman says to Lisa.

"Yup, I'm going to be late. At least it isn't my fault this time," Lisa thinks to herself as she is standing there waiting for the train to start moving again.

Everyone is having various conversations with the people next to them while the train is at a standstill. When suddenly deep inside the transportation tunnel for the train, the lights not only in the tunnel go out but also on the train as well. Screams are heard coming from all over the train causing Lisa to clinch her purse close to her.

"What the hell is going on?" she screams.

The lights on the train start flashing rapidly on and off. Everyone is starting to knock into each other and pushing when Lisa notices something outside of the window coming closer to the train doors.

"Get me off this train!" a man standing near Lisa starts screaming out.

"These people are wyling out," she says to herself when she sees something outside the train window. "What the hell is that? Look out the window everyone!"

Weird and odd shapes start forming outside of the windows causing a massive panic on the train. Transparent lights start looking like shadowy figures swaying from side to side as they slowly move closer to the train.

"HOLY HELL! This train is haunted!" yells a man standing in the middle of Lisa's train car.

One of the figures is glowing a whitish color and looks like an old train conductor with one eye missing and his face appears to have been melted. Swinging what looks like an old key attached to a long linked chain around in a circle. While the other shapes look like just a pair of white menacing eyes and no form around them. These shadowy figures seem to surround the train on all sides but never entering causing a massive eruption of panic and fear.

"Oh shit! Oh shit!" Lisa screams out in fear.

People are still pushing and screaming after seeing the lights still flickering on and off at a rapid pace. Little Lisa is being knocked around like a pinball in a train car full of bumpers.

"Everyone calm down," a woman says from the far end of the train opposite of Lisa. "This is just a temporary situation. The train is not haunted. The lights are just going haywire."

Suddenly the lights stop flickering and turn on completely much to the approval of everyone onboard as they start cheering.

"Finally," Lisa says while finally being able to stand still without bumping off another passenger.

"May I have you attention please? We will be on our way very shortly. The malfunction at the 33rd Street Station has been fixed. Thank you for your patience and understanding during this unscheduled situation. We appreciate your business and continued ridership. Thank you again for traveling with Public Trailways Transportation Services," says the Conductor over the intercom again.

"That's a crock of shit! The more we pay, the more shit breaks causing us riders to suffer!" yelled one angry male passenger.

"Preach on!" yelled another man next to him.

"I can't wait to get off this train," Lisa says to the woman sitting next to her. "Did you see the odd shapes outside the window?"

"No," replied the woman. "What do you mean?"

Looking puzzled and confused about how this woman did not see the lights nor the shadowy figure that resembled an old train conductor is beyond her.

"Oh nothing," Lisa replied to the woman. "Must have been my imagination or something."

The train start moving after a few minutes have passed since the Conductor's last announced much to the praise of the riders. Everyone is clapping and cheering while giving each other high fives. The rest of the ride to 40th and Spellrod Blvd Station is a quiet and uneventful ride.

What seemed like forever on a train ride of eventful situations, the doors open at the 40th and Spellrod Station platform making Lisa rush off the train as soon as the door open.

Rushing off the train and up the exit steps to the bright sunshine that awaits her. "It's no way the gang will believe this story about why I'm late," she says while running through the turnstile and up the steps to street level.

After finally getting to the top of the steps and reaching street level, she starts walking as fast as she can to get to the Mad Gamer Arcade. Lisa looks down at her watch as she's hustling up the street and sees that she isn't as late as she thought she was.

"What's twenty minutes considering all the craziness that's happened," she says to herself.

Walking halfway up the block, she does not notice Marcus walking straight towards her as she is in her own world thinking about what happened to her today.

"Hey Lisa," Marcus yells out while waving his arms.

She looks up to see Marcus walking towards her and waving his arms at her.

"Hey Marcus," she says while he is about four feet away. "You will not believe the day I am having."

"I can only imagine. Janet and Will are waiting at the arcade for us. I only came down to see if I saw you walking up. And here you are."

"Yeah, here I am. I can't wait to tell this story," she replies.

The two start walking back up towards the arcade, Marcus sends Janet a message that he found Lisa, and they are on their way back.

Chapter Four

All Present and Accounted For

The crew of four are all sitting at a local food spot munching on burgers and fries not to far from the arcade they all met up at while listening to Lisa's story as to way she was late.

One of the many burgers joints in the area but are the most notorious on the strip for their colossal burgers and milkshakes. This establishment has won many awards in which they gladly show off on their walls along with the celebrities that have visited their establishment.

The crew are sitting in a booth along one of the many windows facing Spellrod Blvd with Janet and Lisa seating next to the window across from each other, while Marcus sits next to Janet and William next to Lisa, are on the outer seats of the booth.

William is eating his bacon double with cheese and scarfing it down as if he has eaten in a week. Lisa is playing with her fries in the ketchup cup while Marcus is stealing fries off Janet's tray while she gives him the stare of death for taking her fries.

"Excuse me?" Janet says while looking at Marcus who has one of her fries in his mouth with a smirk on his face.

"What? You weren't eating them," Marcus replies.

Picking up a couple of the leftover fries, Janet playfully throws them at Marcus's face but the jokes on her because he catches a few of them in his mouth. Lisa looks up at the two and just shakes her head.

"Were you trying to hit me with those?" Marcus says with a mouthful of fries.

"Funny," Janet says with a grin on her face.

William stops eating his burger just long enough to add to the conversation. "Will you two just kiss and get it over with already? Man!"

"He'd like that to much," she says.

"Hey, I wouldn't complain about it," Marcus responds.

"I bet," Janet replies.

The attention goes back to Lisa and her adventurous day along with the story she just told. William finishes his burger, wipes his mouth, and looks over at Lisa. "That was one hell of a story you told."

"Well, that is why I was late and it was freaky at the same time," Lisa says.

"Well that is crazy. Where's the free oil?" Janet says.

William gives Janet a strange look and Marcus busts out laughing due to what Janet says while William continues with his odd questionable face. During this time, Marcus slides out the booth and takes all the trays over to the trashcan to dump them so he can clear the table.

"She's late and you're worrying about some free sample of oil? What the hell?" William says to Janet.

"That is a little weird Janet," Marcus says walking back from dumping the trays.

"It's just odd how he picked me out of everybody to give

me a free sample. Let alone a four-ounce bottle at that," Lisa says while going in her bag before handing the bottle to Janet across the table.

"Yeah. How freaking *odd*," William says in a sarcastic tone.

"Aww. Are we feeling a tiny bit jealous over there Will?" Marcus says while lightly laughing while sliding back in the booth next to Janet. "It's nothing to be ashamed of homie. Just shows how much you care."

"You wish."

Janet unscrews the top and takes a whiff of the oil before shoving it under Marcus's nose, making him take an impromptu smell of the oil just as he was about to say something to Lisa. "Smell this!"

Marcus starts gasping for air after Janet shoves the oil under his nose after he ends up taking a big whiff of the oil while making the face of something that is too strong in huge doses. Forcing air out of his lungs through his mouth while shaking his head. "That is some strong stuff or I got too much of that stuff at once." Shaking his head. "Now, what I was going to ask you Lisa was about the fence. What's up with that?"

"I don't know. As I said, I was looking at the different designed hedges and then something black just came at me, smashed into the fence, and was gone just that fast. I jumped back into a mailbox, and then some man asked if I was ok," Lisa says.

"So the guy saw nothing when he came to check on you?" Janet questioned Lisa.

"Not a thing."

"You sure you aren't seeing things baby. A guy comes over to ask if you're ok, yet he sees nothing and says nothing about the fence," William responds with a questionable tone.

"I'm fine. I'm not going crazy."

Marcus is just sitting there biting his lip while looking at Janet trying on the oil then turns and looks at Lisa with a blank stare.

"Ok, something hit the fence, and then it fixed itself when the man came to check on you but you clearly saw it was bent outwards as if something slammed into it?" Marcus asks.

"That's what happened. I know I'm not going crazy," Lisa says. "Did you tell them what happened to you Will?"

"Nope."

Janet stops looking out the window to turn to William and asked what Lisa is talking. William just shrugs his shoulders and gives Lisa a look of why did you have to say something about that.

"So what happened with you Will? Janet asked.

"U-Um…what had happened was," William stumbles over his words. "You won't believe me if I told you."

"Try us. Seems to be a weird day going around," Marcus says.

"Man. It's nothing.

"Right," Janet says in a sarcastic tone.

William is just sitting there looking around the table and all eyes are on him waiting for him to tell his side of the mysterious story. Lisa elbows him in the side to get him to talk and to spill the beans.

"Ow woman. You don't have to elbow me. I'll tell them what happened."

Talking a deep breath before starting his story of how he talked to a man who gave him a mysterious flyer that ended up incinerating in his hands.

"I was on my way home after I talked to Marcus after school. You know me, minding my own business when this man stopped me in the middle of the block. Thinking he's just going to give me a flyer to some party or something along those lines.

The crew is looking at William with the intent of hanging on every word he speaks as if his words have them in a trance.

"So I look at the flyer thinking I'm going to see an address and date of the party…none of that anywhere on there. It's basically a blank piece of paper with one sentence written in the middle of the paper."

"Open your mind and accept reality as things are."

"Open your mind and accept reality as things are," Marcus says in a confused tone. "What's up with that creepy shit?"

"That's nothing. The paper starts getting hot while I'm holding it and suddenly it just sparks up into a flame," William says.

"Oh no!" Janet says. "I would have been gone."

"What happened with the man who gave you the flyer?" Marcus asked.

"I have no idea but he wasn't around when that paper sparked up. I had two words…I…"

"I'm gone!" Marcus finishes William's sentence for him.

"No doubt homie!" William says giving Marcus their special handshake across the table.

"These two," Lisa says while shaking her head.

"So what happened on the train Lisa?" Janet asks while rubbing the oil on her wrists. "This stuff is great."

"I swear the train was haunted. I know I saw a ghost train conductor but no one else seen what I saw. I even asked the woman sitting right next to me."

"So you saw a ghost and they just saw lights flashing?" Marcus asked while standing up to stretch his legs out.

"Yes."

"Creepy," Marcus says while looking at Janet look as though she is dazed and confused. "Janet, you ok over there?"

"W-Wha?" Janet says. "Yeah, I'm good."

"Oooh kay. If you say so. Guess that oil really does work."

"Let's get out of here," William says sliding out of the booth while stretching once he's out. "Plus, that oil is going to give me a headache."

Everyone is out the booth and heading for the front door of the burger spot. Marcus is the first one out the door and holds it open for everyone else to walk through.

Once everyone is outside of the burger spot, they are just standing there trying to decide on how to proceed with the next part of the process. The sun is still out for the time being but will be going down in a few hours and there is a slight chill in the evening air. The pavements are becoming more packed with foot traffic as more people are coming out to go to the movie theater and fancy restaurants in the area. The Mad Gamer is also seeing the older 18-25 crowd replacing the younger generation that were in there earlier in the day.

As the gang walks up the street, they walk over to a nearby park and have a seat at one of the many picnic tables that are set up. Janet and Lisa sit on the benches of the table next to each other while Marcus sits across from them and William sits on the table itself next to Marcus.

"So back to you Lisa. What happened when the lights were flickering again?" Janet asked.

"It was crazy. The lights just started flickering and then this figure came up to the glass looking like an old train conductor. Then the train was surrounded by ghosts but they never attempted to come onto the train," Lisa replies.

"Wow!" Marcus says in a surprised tone. "That is straight freaky. Even worst that no one else was able to see it happening."

"I know. It freaked me out."

Marcus clears his throat real fast before he proceeds to add to the story of the day craziness.

"I have something to add that is crazy that happened to me right after I talked to Janet.

Janet's head pops up from looking off into the background at the kids running around the park. "Say what now?"

"Yeah, after I got off the phone with you. I got some random text that said, "Don't Go!"

Janet, Lisa, and William just look at Marcus with a confused look on their faces as if they had just seen a ghost. First William with the incinerating flyer, then Lisa with the bending fence and ghosts on the train haunting, now it's Marcus confessing that something strange has happened to him as well.

"Oh kay now. Don't all stare at me like I have eight eyes popping out my head."

"So what happened to you?" asked Lisa.

"I was getting off the phone with Janet and put my phone down when I got the text. I look at it and it had that message. Okay, no big deal. I just delete that message. Then it just kept coming through non-stop for almost a minute. When it was all said and done, there were about seventy-five messages once it finally stopped."

"And you're just now saying something?" Janet says with a look of concern not only on her face but also in her voice while also sounding a tad bit upset.

The rest of the gang just looks at her in a questionable manner.

"What?"

"Nothing at all," the three of them say while staring in opposite directions.

"Anyway, I have no idea what any of this means and why

Janet is the only one who hasn't had some strange or creepy phenomenon happen to her," Marcus says to the group.

"Don't blame me cause yall got some eerie things happening and I don't," Janet responds. "Yall can keep all that."

"It's still just weird," replied William.

"I wonder what all of this means though," says Lisa.

"Just a bunch of weirdness if you ask me," Marcus says. "Which one of yall got me sucked into your nightmare?"

"Aight Will, what's the catch with this house?" Janet asks.

"Basically, I heard a couple kids talking about a haunted house in our lovely town. One said bums go in and never come out. Supposedly saw someone go in and never came back out."

Marcus adjust the rim on his hat flexing it a few times. "So we're basically here because of a story?"

"Pretty much but then I saw the special on tv and it detailed who the guy was, well who the pirate was."

"And –," is about all Janet could get out before she was cut off by William.

"And his name is; well was, Red Point the Pirate. Captain Blatz, known as "The Viking," a notorious and murderous pirate, adopted Red Point. The special never said what Red Point's real name was. All they know was when he became a pirate; Red Point, also started a murderous killing spree and village pillager."

"So we're going to mess with the pirate's booty by going to this supposedly haunted house," Janet asks.

"Very funny Janet," Lisa says.

“Red Point might have hid gold and his various treasure in our city centuries ago. It’s possible the address that kid gave me where he saw the bums go in and never come out might be that place,” William adds.

“There we have it folks. It’s always a hidden treasure in there somewhere. Why else would anyone want to check out a haunted house that was never in the news,” Janet says while standing up and walking around the table.

“All $35 million dollars’ worth of treasure,” William adds.

The gang pauses and just looks at William as if he was speaking in a different language or an ancient tongue. Their jaws drop to the ground when they hear how much the potential treasure would be worth today.

“Wow. That’s a nice price tag on something that may not be there,” Janet says.

“Especially when this place could just be a hobo den. They could all be in there getting all drugged up,” Marcus adds to go along with what Janet said moments earlier.

“They very well could be,” William says.

“Still can’t believe Lisa had two separate incidences in one day. That is crazy,” said Marcus standing just behind the bench of the table.

“People on the train were saying that the train was haunted but all they saw were the lights flickering off and on. They never even seen what I saw outside the window,” says Lisa. “Can this day get any crazier?”

“Usually when you say that, crazy things happen,” Marcus replies to Lisa’s question.

Janet jumps into the conversation after she finishes smelling the oil she rubbed on her wrists earlier. "So where did you get this from Lisa?"

"The 3rd and Groove Road Station. Funny thing is, when I got on the train and looked for him, he wasn't there. Almost like he just disappeared into thin air."

"No wonder you two are together. People just give you two stuff and disappear," Marcus directs that towards Lisa and William.

"Oh shut up homie," William fires back while laughing.

"So what else should we know about this place Will?" asked Janet.

"Supposedly in 500 years, Red Point is coming back to collect what's his. Highly unlikely considering it's an urban legend and all."

"Where is this p–?"

Before Marcus could finish his sentence, there are screams in the background towards Spellrod Blvd and a car horn honking. The gang gets up from the table quickly and looking down the street towards the Mad Gamer only to see lights flashing and people running in all directions.

The more they look towards Spellrod Blvd; they can see what is causing the commotion, a car is running down the sidewalk out of control while crashing into parked vehicles along the way causing alarms to go off, and in the process causing the car's lights to flash.

They make it to the edge of the park curbside to see a path of destruction carved out by the runaway car when suddenly they hear a loud crash farther down the street. Not far away, they hear the sirens of emergency vehicles coming down the road.

"I hope no one is hurt," says Lisa while interlocking her left arm into William's right arm.

"Well, you did ask what else crazy can happen," says Marcus while looking at Lisa.

As they look at the destruction, two police cars and an ambulance zip past them onto the crash car while another ambulance stops in the middle of the street to check on anyone who was hurt during the situation.

Everyone across the street are dazed and confused as to what just happened. People are talking to other people trying to figure out why are car was on the sidewalk to begin with.

A large crowd is gathering by the crashed car, which came to a complete stop at the end of Spellrod Blvd and Crosswinds Ave after running into the back of a black SUV. The result of the crash completely smashed the entire front end of the car into the front seats of the vehicle with airbags deployed. The damage done to the vehicle after the crash would crush any individual still inside from the waist down, if not killing them instantly upon impact.

The police at the crash scene are pushing everyone far enough away from the car in case it catches fire or worse. A firetruck is coming down Crosswinds Ave and stopping at the corner just before getting to the car to check things out and to give the all clear signal before the cops can investigate the scene.

The car that caused all the ruckus is a four door jade colored sedan with tinted windows and a bunch of bumper stickers all over the trunk and bumper with a sunroof with black door molding on both sides of the car.

Overhearing a conversation between two women who just happened to be standing close to the gang who witnessed what happened, Marcus proceeds to go over and talk to him about what they saw.

"Excuse me ladies. Sorry to interrupt but did you see what happened?"

A pretty redhead with hair a little past her shoulders, green eyes, and freckles proceeds to tell Marcus and the rest of the gang what she witnessed. She tells them that the green colored sedan was in the middle lane of the street before driving onto the sidewalk since traffic was not moving. Started honking the horn to get people to move out the way then once there was no one on the sidewalk, the car gunned the engine and before you know it, the car crashed into the SUV.

"Thank you ladies. Appreciate you filling us in on the situation," says Marcus.

"You're welcome," replies the redhead.

The gang like many others make their way down to the accident scene to see the damage caused by the crash. The firefighters have cleared the scene for any fire and electrical hazards and are bringing over the Jaws of Life to rip the door off the driver's side of the car.

"Ok everyone. Back up please," one of the officers on scene says while moving the crowd farther back.

By this time, it seems like everyone that were on Spellrod Blvd are now standing around the accident scene.

"Fire it up!" yelled one of the firefighters.

With traffic at a standstill, backed all the way up the block, you hear a loud roar as one of the firefighters turns on the Jaws of Life. The Jaws of Life rip through the driver's side door like a hot knife through soft butter. The sound of crunching metal fills the air that echoed to the other end of Spellrod Blvd.

To everyone's surprise especially that of the firefighter who ripped the door off the car, the driver's seat is completely empty. The entire crowd lets out a giant gasp as they are witnessing something they did not think was possible.

"Chief, how is this even possible?" the firefighter holding the Jaws of Life asks his Captain.

"I have no idea. Check the car for blood. It's no way the person walked away without a scratch," the Fire Chief responds.

Marcus, Lisa, Janet, and William all just look at each other in shock that the car is empty considering how bad the car impacted the back of the SUV.

"You just had to ask Lisa," says Marcus looking at Lisa. "There is your crazy."

Lisa just shrugs her shoulders in amazement. "Just when you thought you've seen it all."

"I'm sure this'll be on the news at ten o'clock tonight," said Janet.

"You know it will be," said Marcus. "Can't wait to see how this turns out."

The accident and the resulting circumstances caused a backlog of traffic between 41st and Spellrod Blvd to 45th and Spellrod Blvd is finally allowed to move after a police officer starts diverting traffic to the far left lane only.

Cars are honking now that they are starting to move and people are yelling out of their windows in anger that things took this long to move forward. Most of the drivers had to restart their cars because they have been sitting there for so long and did not want to waste the gas.

Traffic continues to move slowly even after the diversion, due to cars having to cross over to the left lane from the far right and nosey on-lookers of the accident scene.

The large crowd is also starting to disperse now that the traffic is moving and the tow trucks have arrived to take the two cars to the Police impound lot for evidence. Police and firefighters are also continuing to scout the area for the driver of the vehicle while others are taking witness statements.

Chapter Five

And Away They Go

The gang starts to head back up the street to plan their next move as to what to do about the haunted house trip. The ambulances are also moving away from the scene with their lights off to what likely means no one was injured and they do not have to rush anyone to the hospital. Traffic is still jam packed for blocks as moving around the accident scene is a very slow process, with cars having to cut in and out of the three lanes. The remaining citizens in the area that decided to hang around the scene can still be heard talking about the accident and what could have possibly lead up to things happening the way they have.

Stopping at one of the green park bench style seats that sit just outside one of the businesses, Janet and Lisa have a seat while Marcus and William stand just off to the side of them.

"So where exactly are we going anywhere?" asked Marcus who now has his right foot propped up on the edge of the bench.

"According to the kid who I was talking to that day. He said we have to go to 46th and Cannon Way. House number 4655 and that's the house with only one way in," replies William.

"Cannon Way. What is that near?"

"Umm…between…ah….Ridgemore and umm…Turner. It's a little one way street that I think is a dead end," says Janet who smelling her wrist. "This oil is on point and definitely relaxing."

"We know what to get her for a present now," Marcus says.

Janet shoots Marcus a look of death as if she was about to shoot daggers out of her eyes like a machine gun.

Marcus starts to back away from the bench very slowly and in doing so almost backs into one of the trees that line the sidewalk.

"How far from here is Cannon Way?" asked Lisa who has her left leg crossed over her right knee.

Everyone looks at Janet waiting for her to give a timetable for the trip and she looks at them with her eyes going back and forth at the three pair of eyes looking at her while she makes a questionable face.

"What? Why is everyone looking at me?" she says in a questionable tone with a look of confusion on her face.

"How far is the walk to Cannon Way?" asked Lisa again.

Janet takes a second to respond as it looks like she is just staring off into deep space when Marcus comes over and waves his hand in front of her face.

"Huh…oh…it's about 15mins walking. And will you get your hand out of my mouth fool," Janet responds back to Lisa while smacking Marcus' hand out of her face.

Traffic flow is starting to return to normal as the police tow trucks clear the accident scene as they are opening the remaining of the two of three lanes the police blocked off due to the incident.

"You going to be ok Janet? You seem a little out of it," asked Lisa.

"Yeah, why are yall acting like I'm losing my mind or something…"

Before Janet could finish her response to Lisa, she suddenly begins to glow a light blue in her skin tone and her eyes turn a bright yellow causing Marcus, William, and Lisa to jump away from her.

"What the hell!" William says in a shaky voice while still backing away from Janet.

"What's wrong? Why everybody jump away from me?" asked Janet as she is sitting on the bench and oblivious to her sudden transformation.

As people are walking past, they do not seem to notice what is going on with Janet, causing Marcus, William and Lisa to think they are going crazy. As people walk by, they are asking if they see anything strange with Janet, to which they would all reply, "Not at all."

"What is going on?" asked Janet as she sees the others shaking with terror. "Why you do you looked so scared of me?"

Marcus slowly walks over to Janet and touches her shoulder only to pull his hand away quickly as if she was made of fire.

"What the hell is going on?" says Marcus as he backs away shaking his right hand as if it was hot and in pain.

"This day is just getting weirder and weirder with each passing minute. All because you want to see if an urban legend is real. Thanks Will," says Lisa while giving a dirty look at William.

"We still going. This is not stopping anything. She's just blue for now. It'll wear off in no time. So don't go blaming me for everything. You agreed to come."

With each passing second, Janet is turning a darker shade

of blue while her eyes stay a bright yellow in color. She still cannot be touched as her skin and clothing feel like they are on fire. They have no idea what is going on with Janet for all they can do is stand back and look in amazement at how this is even happening to her right now. Still, no one walking by is in no way phased by Janet and her strange glow.

"We have to figure out what is going on with Janet," says Marcus to Lisa and Will. "Ok, so what do we know about the situation?"

"She was fine before Lisa got here. Sarcastic as ever. The usual Janet self but once Lisa got here, we ate, heard her reason for being late and gave her that oil," said William.

"That's it!" says Marcus excitedly. "None of this happened until she put that oil on."

As soon as Marcus finishes his statement, Janet rises from the bench slowly and starts walking towards her three friends with her arms extended in front of her and groaning stopping just inches in front of the three.

"You will not enter! Do not intrude upon the sacred grounds or face the consequences of your actions!" says a ghostly voice coming out of Janet's mouth. She slowly clinches her right fist with her thumb sticking out and slowly slide it across her throat from left to right as if she was cutting her throat.

"Whoa!" says William. "That is freaky!"

As soon as Janet's arms are down by her side, blood starts running down from the invisible cut line from whence she ran her thumb across her throat. "You will not enter! Do not intrude upon the sacred grounds!" she says again in a ghostly and eerie voice.

Blood begins to violently flow from Janet's neck and

completely covering her clothing while the three are just watching this event unfold not knowing what to do to help. As the blood continues to gush out of Janet's neck and down her clothing to the concrete below. Marcus grabs ahold of Janet's neck to attempt to stop the bleeding with blood getting all over his clothes and hands. Lisa and William start running up and down the block in opposite directions trying to get help. Asking people who are walking by, to which through the eyes of the general public, the three seem crazy because there is nothing wrong going on. To the average passerby, they see the three friends as a group of people acting a little weird outside in the crisp cool air.

With Janet collapsed on the cool concrete bleeding out from her neck wound, the three friends are franticly searching for help from anyone who will listen to them. People reacted to their attempts for help with pushes and weird looks on their faces.

"Please help my friend! She's bleeding out on the concrete!" yelled Marcus at the top of his lungs while still applying pressure to Janet's neck.

A young woman stopped and looked at Marcus as if she was going to help only for Marcus to hear her say, "There is no one there buddy. What are you smoking?"

"Smoking! My friend is lying here bleeding and you ask me what I'm smoking!" he yelled back at the young woman while looking up at her. "UGH!" To which the young woman quickly walks away just as fast as she stopped to speak to him.

"Janet! Janet!" yelled Marcus while still applying pressure to her neck. "Come on. This can't be happening right now."

William and Lisa come running back towards Marcus out of breath and kneeling next to him and Janet. The look on their faces is one of disbelief and sorrow about the events of today.

Janet still laid out on her back with Marcus applying pressure to stop the bleeding with passersby continuing to look at them as if they are having a drug-induced episode.

"Can't believe this is happening!" yelled Lisa who is pacing back and forth next to Janet's head. "Why is this happening?"

"Like we know. If we knew the answer to this, we might not be in this situation," says William sounding distressed who is now sitting on the ground with his hands on his head.

Looking back at the bench behind the group of friends sits Janet who seems to be in a haze from the oil she inhaled from Lisa. Slowly starting to shake her head while her eyes are blurry and blinking constantly, she can barely make out three people sitting on the ground in front of her. As she leans forward, she holds her head as if she has a severe migraine and rubbing her eyes trying to get the blurriness to subside. After rubbing her eyes for a few seconds, she is able to see Marcus, Lisa, and William sitting on the ground crying and sobbing.

"Hey!" Janet yells over to the three while still sitting on the bench trying to gain her bearings. "Why are you on the ground like that?"

The three continue to sit on the ground as if they did not hear what she said to them. People are still looking at the three, as they were a freak show clown act from a circus. Others are just walking by as if they were just there sitting on the sidewalk in the middle of a busy day. Paying no attention to the situation of three people acting rather strangely.

"Hey!" Janet yells to them once again while trying to stand but her legs are shaking while she's holding onto the bench. "Whoa. Let me sit back down for a minute."

As Janet sits back down, she can hear the rest of her friends screaming and crying in agony. From what she can see, Marcus is holding his own hand screaming, "Don't die Janet!" at the top of his lungs with Lisa and William on each side of him sitting on the ground.

"Why does this fool think I'm dead? Why in the hell is he holding his own hand? Something is definitely wrong here."

Janet slowly shakes her head trying to clear the fog of cobwebs so she can attempt to stand. About five minutes of just staring at Marcus, Lisa and William screaming and sobbing on the sidewalk, she is able to regain her balance and is able to walk over to the others.

"Hello," she says standing right behind Marcus. "Can you hear me?"

There is no response from anyone. Still feeling light headed, she again tries to get their attention by waving her hand in front of their faces. Much to no avail but not for lack of her efforts. As a last resort, she proceeds to smack Marcus hard upside the back of his head hard causing him to snap out of whatever trance that was consuming his psyche.

"YOO! Who the hell smacked me in the head?" yelled Marcus while rubbing the back of his head.

"I did," proclaimed Janet.

Marcus turned around after hearing Janet's voice with the biggest confused look on his face but manages to jump up and give her the biggest hug he could possible give to anyone. Thinking he was holding her dying body in his arms just a few seconds ago, his eyes start tearing up so badly.

"I swore I was holding your dead body in my arms a

second ago. What happened?" asked Marcus.

"I have no idea. I just started feeling funny and I don't even know what happened the last few minutes."

"What about these two?" questioned Marcus well still rubbing his head.

"Smack them in the head like I did you. You get William and I'll pop Lisa in the head."

"They do look silly as hell just sitting there crying over nothing."

"Let's not forget you were just sitting there with them Marcus before I smacked you in the head."

"Funny. Let's wake them up," he says while making a sarcastic face at Janet.

The two get into position with everyone just walking past them while still giving them weird stares. William and Lisa are now side by side still thinking Janet is deceased in their minds.

"You sure we can't leave them like this for a little bit longer?" asked Marcus while pulling out his cellphone.

"If you don't put that phone away! Don't make me smack you again."

"Fine," he says with a sigh in his voice. "It would have been funny though."

"Just smack William upside the head so we can get this over with and everyone can stop looking at us like we are some deranged morons."

The two get behind their respective heads and prepare to

smack the two out of their trance. People are now stopping to look at the four and their crazy situation. As weird as things are, the people seem to think this is some kind of performance piece. They are now standing around anticipating the next move of the performance.

"Um…why is everyone standing around staring at us now?" asks Marcus while speaking out the side of his mouth.

Janet starts shifting her eyes left to right and back again while having a confused look on her face. "I have no idea but let's hurry up and get out of here."

"Copy that."

Just as Janet and Marcus are preparing to smack the back of Lisa and William's head respectively, someone from the back of the crowd yells out.

"This is one of the best sidewalk shows ever!" yelled some random person from the back of the gathered crowd.

Then another and another start clapping as though they knew that what they perceived as a performance was ending soon. Marcus and Janet start looking at each other smiling. Some of the very same people who were walking up the street ignoring the situation are now the very same people in passing who are stopping and clapping.

Janet smacks Lisa in the back of her head and the surrounding crowd goes crazy followed by Marcus smacking William, making the crowd go crazier. Janet and Marcus look at each other to see if it worked as it did for him and just shrug their shoulders. Lisa and William are still in a trance sitting next to each other still sobbing seemingly unaffected by the smacks they took to the back of their heads.

"Now what do we do?" he whispers over to Janet.

"I have no idea. It was almost instant with you."

"They are going to be embarrassed when they snap out of this."

"Right. Smack him again Marcus."

"Ok," he replies as he raises his hand to smack William in the head again a little harder than last time.

This time it seems to work on William as he lets out a loud cry of pain and quickly reaches for the back of his head and starts rubbing the spot where Marcus just hit him. The surrounding crowds erupts again, making William jump up from off the ground and yell at the crowd.

"What the hell is going on?" yells William as he turns and looks at Marcus and Janet. "What the hell? I thought you were dead."

"Apparently you weren't the only one," said Janet while pointing to Lisa.

"What's wrong with her?" asked William as he turns to look over at Lisa. "And why is my head hurting?"

"She's in a trance or something. Only way that seems to snap her out of it is to smack her in the back of the head," said Marcus.

"So that's why my head is stinging," says William while rubbing his head. "What's up with the crowd?"

"They either think we're on drugs or performing a street play," says Janet.

"Ok! Break it up! The show is over!" yelled William to the surrounding crowd.

The crowd starts moaning in disgust and walking away slowly. William kneels down next to Lisa and puts his arms around her.

"How can we fix this?" William asked.

"That's your girl homie. Maybe she'll snap out of this funk if you give her a kiss or something," says Marcus.

"This isn't some Sleeping Beauty story time crap," Janet sarcastically says.

"This is what I looked like? Staring off into space like nothing is going on upstairs?"

"Pretty much homie."

"Here goes nothing."

William leans over and kisses Lisa on her lips hoping that will snap her out of the trance.

"Did it work?" asked Marcus.

Minutes seem to go by without any results when suddenly Lisa falls over on the concrete onto her back and starts twitching.

"The hell kind of kissing you giving out? The kiss of death?" Janet says in a sarcastic tone.

"Real funny Janet," replied William.

A few more minutes go by before Lisa opens her eyes and sits up on her own power while holding her head.

"What happened to me?" Lisa asked while holding her

head and looking over at Janet with a surprised look on her face.

"Hey Lisa. Yeah, I am not dead how everyone thought I was. I have no idea what happened but I'm still alive and kicking," says Janet.

"Well, it looks like the oil you gave Janet had some adverse side effects on not only her but us as well," says Marcus.

They all go back a few steps and sit on the bench in front of the arcade where this trip was the starting point of this adventure to the haunted house.

"So when I came to, the three of you were all on your knees on the ground crying like someone died. Come to find out from Marcus that person was I. Now what happened, I have no idea whatsoever," says Janet.

"Well it looks like you were changing colors and then you did the slit your throat motion and then seconds later blood started gushing out of your neck. Then you said something about, "Don't Go!" or something like that and then you dropped to the ground," says Marcus.

"Whoa, now that's freaky," replied Janet. "No wonder yall were on the ground when I came around. Then the crowd started forming and that's when I smacked Marcus in the head."

"Ol heavy handed ass. My head still stinging," said Marcus while rubbing his head.

"Funny. How are you feeling Lisa?" Janet asked intently.

"I still feel a little funny but slowly getting back to normal."

The foursome are just sitting on the bench trying to regain

their wits about them while watching everyone walk by enjoying their night out on the town. The temperature is getting a little cooler in the crisp night air of downtown Starside. After the events of the car accident and the situation with Janet, only a mere hour has passed since the start of all the confusion.

The group sits at the bench for an additional ten minutes before deciding on their next move. After today's events, they need to regain some of their sanity before continuing.

"Everyone good?" William asked.

The three all nod their head in agreement.

"So now what do we do?" Marcus sparked the topic of conversation.

It does not take long before William fires back a quick response to Marcus' question before anyone else could even manage to move their lips.

"I want to know this place is real. So I say let's keep going even after all of this madness," replied William.

"Figures you would say that," Lisa chimes in while getting up off the bench. "You just want that treasure."

"Sue me," William fires back while smiling at Lisa.

"I'm good so if we are still going then let's go. It's not that late so we can roll out and be back before eleven," says Marcus.

All eyes turn to Janet as they await her decision on whether to keep going or to go home and forget this day ever happened.

"Come on Janet. You know you want to go check this place out," says William.

"I don't know. After everything that has happened today. This is some freaky and creepy stuff I wasn't planning on," Janet replies.

"We're only ten or so minutes away walking. We've come this far so why not finish this," says Marcus.

"True. We might as well finish this," Janet replies. "Let's go see this urban legend in our very own city."

"And before we go, throw away that crazy oil you got from the mystery train man," says Marcus.

"Definitely," replied Lisa.

Janet goes into her pocket and pulls out the container of oil and starts walking over to the trashcan that is several feet away tucked under a sidewalk tree. Moments later, the three hear a loud clanging sound as Janet throws the oil forcefully into the side of the trashcan.

"Good riddance," Janet yells out before turning back to walk to the group. "So we out or what?"

"Let's go," declares William excitedly.

"I still say this is a bad idea but that's just my two cent," replies Lisa.

"Your two cents have been noted and deposited into the Bank of Let's Go," William jokingly says back to Lisa. "Everything will be fine baby. I got you."

Marcus and Janet just look at each and start laughing but stop as soon as William turns around and looks at the pair. William shoots them an evil look causing Janet to make a pointing motion over towards Marcus.

"Really Janet?"

"What?"

"Will you two come on!" William yells back to Janet and Marcus who are thirty feet behind him.

The rest of the walk to the house is quiet with a couple of jokes thrown in to break up the silence other than the noise of traffic during the cool night stroll.

Chapter Six

The Arrival

The four friends arrive in the general area of where they think the haunted house would be located on Cannon Way. The area around them are just empty lots of overgrown weeds, uncut grass, and condemned buildings that are hollow shells of their former selves down the skinny two way street. Even the street on this dead end block has several large potholes littered all up and down the road. The sidewalks are massive cracks and uplifted concrete slabs on both sides of the path. Graffiti litters every inch of available wall space that are still standing. As they approach the 4655 address, a cold breeze blows forcefully, stopping the group of friends dead in their tracks.

"Whoa! That was cold," says Janet while still shaking.

"See, it's a sign telling us not to go. What more do you need of a warning?" Lisa says while looking concerned.

Several of the streetlights start flickering off and on several times before remaining dimly lit.

"Well if that isn't slightly creepy," says Marcus.

"What a punk. It is about that time for streetlights to turn on. We are in an old part of the city. Surprised they even work at all," replied William.

They are standing in front of what would be 4655 Cannon Way, the haunted house of urban legend at the end of the dead end block. The house is a condemned three story white painted colonial home with a slanted brown roof that are supported by tall painted chipped white columns that reach the second floor of the building. There is also a wraparound porch with an archway for an entrance before proceeding to the tall cracked wooden front door flanked by two windows on each side. Tattered brown ripped curtains hang from the interior of the broken windows that do not seem affected by the cool breeze blowing. There are six steps that lead up to the withered broken porch that houses exposed nails and splintered wood shooting from the floor. A crisscrossing pattern wooden lattice covers the lower crawl space under the porch which prevents various creatures from living underneath of the house.

"This place doesn't look haunted besides the fact we're on a dead end street with no traffic and basically standing in an abandoned lot. No wonder bums come here and aren't seen again," says Janet.

"Creepy place to die," replies Lisa.

"Oh stop worrying baby. You know I won't let anything happen to you," says William while walking over to hug Lisa.

"Uh huh."

"So…who wants to go first?" Marcus asked of the group.

Everyone turns and looks at William to make the first move.

"Why is everyone looking at me?" questioned William.

"Well, this was your idea to begin with. On top of that, you got us to come with you. So, you should do the honors of walking on up there and checking things out," said Marcus.

William starts walking back and forth in front of the run down wooden steps of the house with his hands on his hips.

"I have a better idea. We'll let the women go first," he says with a devilish grin on his face with a slight laugh afterwards.

"What a bunch of punks. Suppose to be-,"

Janet can only get so far before Lisa cuts her off mid-sentence.

"Can't even go first to protect us women. Bunch of suckas if you ask me."

"Oh calm down baby, I was just joking. Sheesh. People can't take a joke nowadays," replied William.

"Come on William. We'll both go. Hell, if bums walked up here then we should be able to," says Marcus.

"Ok."

"Besides, what the worst that could happen?" Marcus asks of the group while looking nervously at the steps.

"Falling on your ass onto a splinter," said Janet while laughing a little.

Marcus sends Janet a sarcastic look in her direction while shaking his head.

"Ok. Here goes nothing," William says while placing one foot on the first step checking to see how sturdy it is.

After seeing William standing on the steps, Marcus walks up towards the porch while the wooden decaying planks squeak with each step.

"Well look who decided to join me," William says with a sarcastic tone. "Now are you ladies coming to the party or what?"

"Real funny homie," Marcus replies. "So who's next to join us?"

Janet and Lisa just look at each other before taking a deep breath and proceed to walking up the squeaking wooden steps of the dilapidated house.

"Come on Lisa. How bad can it be? No way we let these guys try to clown us for being scared. I know that won't be happening with me. You're my girl so I can't let that happen."

The moment Lisa places her foot onto the first step; it immediately creates a loud cracking noise causing Lisa to jump back in fear. Janet then takes Lisa's hand in support before proceeding again up the steps while Marcus and William await up top with their arms folded and appear to be waiting impatiently.

"It's ok, you got this," Janet reassures Lisa.

"Yeah, thank you Janet."

The two walk hand in hand up the creaky and crackling steps going one at a time until they reach the porch where Marcus and William are awaiting them.

"What took you ladies so…"

Before William could finish his statement, the porch begins to shake and buckle under the weight of the four of them standing together by the front door. With the sudden shift of the decompressing porch, William and Marcus slammed into the walls by the front door. Lisa, who is not able to maintain her balance, slams into a pillar by the steps to the right. Janet, on the other hand is able to maintain her balance and stand firm but not without a little wobbling from side to side.

"Is everyone ok?" Marcus asks of the group.

“So far,” replied Janet.

“Same here,” said Lisa.

Seeing William peeking in one of the run down broken and cracked windows, Janet calls out to him to see if he is ok.

“William? You ok over there?” Janet asks.

William is too busy to even notice he was being asked a question as he continues to peer inside the window trying to get a better view of the insides of the creepy house.

“Huh? Say what?” William finally responds to the question asked by Janet.

“Are you ok moron?” Janet asks William again.

“Y-Yeah. I’m fine,” he replies back while still looking in the window.

Everyone is dusting himself or herself off from almost going through the floor of the porch, while William is peering into the window at whatever he sees inside of the rundown house. Janet, Lisa, and Marcus all walk over to get a better glimpse at whatever William has fixated on for so long. Only to see nothing but dusty cloth covered furniture and a ton of cobwebs hanging from the two visible chandeliers and dangling over the window.

Backing away from the window, William has a smirk on his face. “So which one of yall had the extra donut for breakfast this morning?”

“Real funny smartass,” Lisa responds with a sarcastic tone while shooting William an evil look in the process. “Step on up, it’s safe he says. Won’t be listening to you no more.”

“Sue me lady…”

William stops in the middle of his sentence because he thought he heard a strange noise coming from inside of the house.

"Did any of you hear that noise?" William asked with eyes wide open.

Marcus can't help but take a step back and just looks at William like he is crazy. "Hear what? Stop acting like a punk and open the door."

"No, I know I heard something. Hell, you open the door."

"Stop playing William," Lisa says while sounding a little scared.

"I'm getting real sick of you two punks. Move out of my way!" Janet says while moving towards the front door.

Janet gets to the front door to turn the knob, only to find the door is locked from the inside. She shakes the handle to see if the knob is just jammed but to no avail.

"So much for that option," Janet says.

"Nicely done there Janet," Marcus replies with sarcasm in his voice. "Couldn't have done that better myself."

"Shut up Marcus!"

Marcus starts laughing before asking William what he thinks he heard coming from inside of the house.

"So what did you hear?" Marcus asked William.

"Funny. It was a weird howling sound. Not like a wolf but I little bit different."

"Well it is an old house with a bucket load of cracks and

holes so that's no surprise with this crazy wind blowing," Janet replies.

"It wasn't the wind. I know what that sounds like."

"Such a man you are. Scared of a little wind passing through an old house," Janet responds with a little smirk on her face.

"Ha ha ha. I'm so glad you're able to get a laugh out of this situation. You know your ass is just as scared. No need to act tough around us. So don't go grabbing me if something happens and you get scared once we're inside this place," William responds back sounding a little upset.

Janet can't help but bust out laughing at what William just said to her. "In your dreams buddy. That's about the only place that would happen."

"So how are we getting in?" Lisa asked breaking the silence after Janet stopped laughing.

"The same way everyone else does…we'll ring the door bell," replies Marcus.

Janet just rolls her eyes at Marcus.

"What a fool," William says back at Marcus. "I'll kick that shit in."

Everyone just starts laughing at William for saying something so absurd. The front door is far from flimsy and appears to be of a thicker wood that has managed to last as long as it has over the years.

"I got ten bucks on the door. Who else wants in on this action?" Marcus says while sounding like a bookie.

"I'll take that action. Gimmie fifteen on the door!" Janet says while reaching in her pockets and pulling out three five dollar bills and waving them around.

Lisa can't help but stand on the side trying hard to not laugh out loud.

"Assholes!" William says with a bit of sarcasm.

"So go ahead and do your thing homie," Marcus says.

"No doubt."

Everyone backs up from not only the door but William as well as he plants his foot onto the door to get a good angle for his kick.

"See, you gotta kick it right in the handle to break the frame," said William as he starts mumbling to himself while backing away from the door before he attempts to kick it in.

"Don't hurt yourself baby," Lisa sounding concerned for William's ill-advised plan to kick down the door.

"I'll be fine. Just wait and see," William responds back.

William takes three steps back to the very edge of the porch to get a good running start while Marcus and Janet just look at each other with anticipation of a complete disaster on his part.

William starts his frontal assault on the front door and within kicking distance of the door; he raises his leg to prepare for impact. Just as soon as he is within a foot from kicking the door, it slowly creeps open causing William to stop dead in his tracks with a surprised look on his face. As the door is opening, everyone just looks at each other in fear and agony as a horribly loud shrieking noise coming from the opening makes the friends cover their ears in pain. Suddenly, a cold breeze shoots out of the now fully opened front door leaving the friends even more terrified than they already were.

“What the hell was that?” Lisa says in a terrified tone.

“Cold breeze and creaky opening doors. I can only imagine what that could mean,” Janet says.

“Maybe this place is haunted for real.”

“Really Lisa? There is no such thing as something being haunted,” William responds back to her.

“Still willing to go first Ms. DeMay? Or did all that bravery just disappear when the cold breeze blew and the door opened?” Marcus asks of Janet.

Janet just looks at William with a smirk on her face and tries to put on a brave face while standing between the window and the front door on the left side. William is still standing directly in front of the door still surprised at what happened before he kicked in the door.

“Um…Yeah. There’s no such thing as ghosts,” Janet replies with her voice sounding a little shaky.

Standing just off to the right side of the door but closer to the steps, Marcus is standing there with his arms crossed closer to the railing of the steps. “Be my guest. However, given your ancestral background, I’d figure you’d think a little differently.”

“It’s just that, my ancestral background. It doesn’t prove that everything is a haunting,” Janet replies.

“You’re braver than me,” Lisa says.

“Soooo William…are you just going to stand there or are

you going to go in?"

William turns to respond to Janet when he hears something moving around inside the house causing him to jump back and land in front of Marcus.

"What was that?" Lisa asked. "I knew this wasn't a good idea. Should have just stayed home after the day I had."

"Told you I heard something in the house. It's too late to turn back now Lisa. You're already here now. Plus, you wouldn't want to miss out on all the fun," William replied.

"Tell me you got some flashlights in that bag of yours William or something to give us some light?" Marcus asked while walking towards the front door.

"Of course, I told you I have a bag full of stuff," William says while digging in the bag before tossing a flashlight over to Marcus.

Marcus catches the flashlight in mid-air with his right hand before hitting the button and blasting a bright beam of light into the decrepit house. The light is exposing even more of the dusty and old contents of the house. The rest of the gang comes over to have a peek inside the house.

"You see anything?" Lisa asked who is standing behind William who is standing in front of the door.

"Nothing. So who wants to go in first? Give everyone a flashlight Will."

William hands out the other two flashlights before taking one himself. The remaining beams of light brighten the interior of the house while the gang observed the scene. Each beam illuminates a different area of the living room that sits just on the inside of the front door.

“I have a few more things in this bag for us to use. They will come in handy just for cases like these,” William said. He then starts digging into his bag of goodies and begins pulling out dust mask.

“Oh yeah!” Janet says with excitement. “These will definitely come in handy.”

‘Who knows how contaminated this dust can be,” William said while handing out the mask before placing one over his face.

“I have no idea how the homeless stayed in this place,” Lisa said.

“Well, when you have nowhere to go, a place like this is like a palace,” Janet replies.

“True.”

The gang proceeds to put on their dust mask so they no longer have to inhale the dust filled aired around them before entering the abandoned home. The stale air continued to creep out of the house along with dust circulating through the front door.

After placing his dust mask over his face, Marcus continues peeking into the house while shining his flashlight inside. The floating dust particles fill the light emanating from the bright beam of the flashlight. The air contains a stale mildew scent that flew out of the house as soon as the door flung itself open before William tried kicking in the door.

“Ok, this is some stank ass air. Good thing you bought these masks Will,” Marcus says.

“I may not be a boy scout but you know I always come

prepared to all occasions."

"Good one Will. You must be dreaming again."

"The best you'll never know about Janet."

"Eww!"

Janet proceeds to walk over to the front door while turning on her flashlight and shining the beam into the surrounding area of the living room in order to check out the eerie interior. The tattered and ripped curtains are blowing in the breeze from the cracked windows and the now opened front door. The dust on the old worn and dirty carpet, completely covered in a thick layer of dust and debris, there would be no way to determine if anyone if ever was walking around the interior of the decrepit house. Just as Janet is prepared to take the lead and walk into the dusty, stank and decrepit home, Marcus grabs her by the arm.

"What are you doing?"

"I'm going in. We are all just standing here while the sun is going down. So we doing this or yall punking out?"

Marcus just looks at Janet and releases her arm. "Let's do this then!"

The two do their special handshake and end it with a hug and a salute to each other before proceeding to enter the house.

Chapter Seven

Knock Knock

Everyone is just standing there with his or her flashlights shining into the living room of the house without anyone attempting to enter the home. Janet prepared herself to enter through front door to lead the pack. Instead, hesitated just before entering so she could psyche herself up to shake the nerves.

"Oh, look who got cold feet after talking all that trash," William says sarcastically to Janet.

"Shut up Will! I'm going unlike you!" Janet snaps back. "I'm going in."

Janet shines her light down toward the threshold of the front door frame and then towards the inside of the house before entering. The remaining three are just looking on with anticipation as to what may happen next. Janet steps into the doorway over the threshold of the entrance with her right foot landing just on the inside of the house. No longer than a split second later, her left foot is touching down on the inside of the house that the floor buckled causing her to fall to her knees in shock with a bloom of dust kicking up into the air.

"Ahh!" Janet screams out.

Marcus looking down inside the entrance to see Janet down on her knees. "Are you ok? I'm coming in to get you."

"Yeah, just watch your step. The floor is weak," Janet replies while slowly getting up of the carpet and dusting herself off while checking for damage. "Good thing I didn't wear my new sneakers for this adventure."

"I knew this wasn't a good idea. I should have just stayed home…," Lisa says sounding a little scared and shaking before being cut off by William.

"And what? Just be bored out of your mind. We're all here now so there is no point in turning back. So let's do this!"

"Sure thing Boss. At least I wouldn't be here dealing with this craziness," Lisa fires back at William.

"Will you two just shut it up, please! I-I'm the one who fell in this dust pit," Janet says while coughing from the excess dust in the air.

"Are you ok Janet? That is the main question," Marcus asked while stepping over the buckled floor section just inside of the doorway.

"No dammit!" Janet replies while shining the flashlight towards her hand. "I chipped my damn nail. If one of you two would have been man enough to step up, I wouldn't have chipped my nail."

William shines his flashlight in Janet's direction while watching her get up off the dusty and dirty carpet. "All this over a chipped nail? You're lucky it wasn't a broken ankle."

"You obviously have no idea how painful a chipped nail can be."

"Nope," William replied.

Lisa and William make their way into the house once Marcus finished helping Janet up from the carpet. The two fanning away the dust as they continually scan the room with their flashlights hitting every inch of the room.

"This dust is crazy. Should have put some goggles in the bag as well," William says.

"Just be happy you weren't the one who fell into the rat trap of dust. I walked all the way here and damn near broke a nail. What kind of crap is this? We are doing whatever to check this place out, and then getting the hell out of here," Janet says in an angry tone.

Lisa lets out a big sneeze as all the dust floating around the room affects her.

"Bless you," Marcus says.

"Thank you. Can we see what we came to see so we can get out of here? This place just looks run down and in no way haunted," Lisa says.

"Yeah well. I looked this place up on the internet before we all got together. So let's just say it's in no way possible that this should be true," Marcus says while everyone is turning around looking at him as he walks farther into the dusty living room.

"What do you mean you looked this place up?" Lisa asked.

"Basically everything Will said about the kids and the show is all true. This house strangely enough has been around since the 15th century. There were crazy amounts of stories online about this place. Granted you can't believe everything you read online but a lot of the historical links somewhat confirmed everything."

"So the gold is real?" William asked with greedy anticipation.

"The 15th century? How is that even possible?" Lisa asked.

"I don't know but that's what pretty much every source reported as far as the aging of the house and the gold is concerned," Marcus replies.

"So let's get paid if this thing about hidden gold is true," William says while rubbing his hands together with a look in his eyes of a mischievous devil.

"Now we're on a treasure hunt? You really believe this is true?" Janet asks every one of the other three.

"Look. Whatever they said before they were hung, the reports said it translated to them coming back and taking what is theirs or if someone disturbed their treasure. So what Will heard on the show is what I read online from various websites."

"Quit playing Marcus," Lisa says sounding a little scared.

"So we are supposed to believe a website from a bunch of conspiracy theorist and crackpots? Some. Not all websites are faker than a four-dollar bill with my face on them," Janet says.

Everyone is now standing around a dusty cloth covered couch centered inside of the living room that sits in front of an old fireplace with a dusty painting hanging a few feet above the mantle.

"So if this is all true, how is it no one else is here? How is this house still standing and not condemned?" Lisa asked.

"You do know this sound like something a parent would tell their kids to scare the crap out of them while camping, right?" Janet says.

"Right? An Urban Legend Janet."

"So where's the gold? This trip just got more interesting,"

William comments with his eyes getting big.

"Hell if I know," Marcus says while shining his flashlight up at the painting. "Hell, ask this guy if he knows anything."

"So where is everyone else? If we heard of this place and the supposed gold. How come no one else is here now?" Janet says while walking away from the group to look around the rest of the living room area.

"Isn't it obvious? They either died here and the house ate them or they were never here to begin with," Marcus replied.

"I don't care! Let's get paid!" William says while also walking away from the fireplace with Lisa following close behind and holding onto the back of his shirt.

Marcus is the only one still standing in front of the fireplace while his flashlight continues to shine on the mysterious painting that hangs above the mantle.

"Do you really think someone died here? No one said anything about dying or seeing dead bodies. After what I saw today, that's enough for me to want to just go home and hide under the covers," Lisa says.

"It'll be fine baby. Just relax. Nothing has happened since we've been here. Could just be more urban legend talk. No big deal," William reassures Lisa.

"Still would like to know what happened to all the homeless people who ventured into this dark and dusty hellhole," Marcus questioned. "So if anyone did go missing in this house, I wonder if this place is booby trapped."

Lisa begins to walk back over towards Marcus, who is still standing by the couch, when she notices how dark it has gotten outside since they have entered the house. As she begins to walk closer to the door, it suddenly slams shut forcefully as if someone or something slammed it on purpose. A force so powerful that the house shook violently upon closing with the return of the cold breeze filling the room.

"What the hell!" Janet turns quickly to face the door with her heart racing.

"Get me out of here, NOW!" Lisa screams at the top of her lungs.

Upon the door slamming shut, a huge bloom of dust shoots up into the air that completely covers their masks. To make matters even worst for the four friends, all of their flashlights begin to flicker off and on rapidly.

"Oh hell! Now what?" William yelled out. "What's going on with our lights?"

"And that cold breeze," Marcus added. "Hope that don't mean a ghost is floating around here."

"You've been watching too many ghost shows…," Janet says before hearing Lisa scream.

"AHHH!" Lisa screamed out. "Something is crawling on my arm!" She says while brushing her left arm frantically while jumping around.

William and Janet come running over to Lisa while still trying to get their flashlights to work properly but managing to shine the flickering light onto Lisa's arms.

"There is nothing on your arm lady," William says to Lisa.

"I swear I felt something crawling on my arm."

"What did it feel like?" Marcus asks.

"Like a spider or something. I just know it was something crawling on my arm."

"I don't see anything on the ground but with all this dust down here, it's kind of hard to see anything on the floor," Marcus says while shining his flickering flashlight onto the floor.

"What a girlie girl," William says.

"Have a heart Will. You see she's shaken up by this," Janet says while hugging Lisa.

"Yeah well. Some gold coins will change her mood in a heartbeat."

"Oh shut up Will!" Janet yells.

The cold air dissipates as fast as it appeared causing the flashlights to return to normal usage and shine bright in the dusty and dark home.

"How weird was that situation?" Marcus asked. "Is everyone good? We all need to calm down."

Marcus walks over to the front door in which they entered only to find out that it's sealed tight. As if the door was never opened and locked from the outside. After several tugs on the handle, Marcus gives up and looks down at his watch.

"This door isn't budging. On top of that, we have another problem," Marcus says.

"What's that?" Lisa asked.

"My watched stopped. Maybe this place is haunted."

The others also check their watch to notice that theirs has also stopped at the exact same time as Marcus' watch. There is no rhyme or reason for the stoppage of time since each member of the group all have different watches from different companies.

"Damn! Mines stopped too!" Janet yells out loudly.

"What's going on with this house? All of our watches stopping at the same time is not a coincidence," William replied.

"Something is definitely not right here," Lisa says while walking closer to William.

"You think?" William answers back in a sarcastic tone.

Janet shines her light in William's eyes as she shoots him an evil look after that remark to Lisa. She then turns her head slightly to the right while raising her eyebrows to signaling for him to knock it off and to leave Lisa alone. In retaliation to Janet's face, William puts the flashlight under his chin and sticks his tongue out at Janet while winking.

"Will you two knock it off already? We have to find a way out of here," Marcus says to the two of them.

"Not before we find that loot those pirates left behind," Will replied. "Where is it supposed treasure anyway?"

Marcus starts walking to the side of the house where the dining room is located while running into cobwebs and sneezing from the dust covering the entire house in that area. Swinging his flashlight left and right trying to find another door to get out of the house. In the dining room is a long table that looks to seat ten people with chairs, dust covered painting and pictures align the walls. There are place settings on the table with silverware included, a big china style cabinet in the upper left corner of the room, two big four squared windows set equally spaced along the back wall, and another door, which looks to lead to the possible kitchen to the right of where he stands.

"This place is beyond dusty. Definitely one too many cobwebs floating around this place," Marcus says.

William walks over to the dining room where Marcus is standing. "Man, where is the treasure in this place?"

"Like I know…the basement," Marcus responds with sarcasm in his voice. "Not like this place has a floor map like the mall with an X marking the treasure on the C-level next to lingerie and electronics."

William begins running back and forth through the living room and dining room looking for a way to get to the basement level. Everyone else just fixes their light on him while shaking their heads. As William hears the laughter from the others, he continues to search the walls for a switch or a doorway.

"If you don't calm your crazy ass down," Janet shouted at William.

William turns and looks over his shoulder.

"I may be crazy but in the end, I'll be a rich crazy person," William responds.

All Marcus could do was shake his head. "When they come back, don't punk up and run."

"No one is scared of some pirate ghosts that don't exist," William replied.

Janet walks back into the living room but not before telling William how scared he really is about attacking ghosts coming to take back their stolen treasure. After a few minutes, Lisa leaves to join Janet in the living room. Leaving Marcus and William in the other room while they continue to search for a way downstairs.

Janet and Lisa proceed to walk into the hallway next to the right side of the living room and down a hall to a smaller room in the upper right corner of the first floor.

Janet walks into the room with her flashlight focusing back and forth before walking over to a dust-covered sheet, which appeared to be covering a chair.

"Damn, this is dusty. Makes me wish I didn't take this cover off so fast," Janet says while pulling off the sheet.

"That's a nice chair," Lisa responds while shining her flashlight on the now exposed chair. "A little odd for it to look so nice and have this much dust covering the sheet."

The room appears to have been a medium sized den with floor to ceiling bookshelves on two of the walls, a desk in the middle of the room, with two lounge style chairs on each side of a small coffee table, and paintings on the right wall and a window to the left opposite of the paintings.

"So true. That is a little weird," Janet says. "Take a look at these paintings."

Janet shines her flashlight on the large painting on the wall.

"I wonder who he is."

Lisa walks over to where Janet is standing to look at the painting with her before brushing away the dust from the nameplate of the painting.

"His name was…William P. Burkehardt. Whoever he is. I'm surprised this painting is still here. Even though it's covered in dust and dirt. Then again, that might be a rcason why no one decided to remove this hideous painting with a creepy looking man," Lisa says.

"He might be related to William."

"Now that would be funny and creepy at the same time."

Continuing to look around the den style room, Janet feels a cold chill come over her body.

"Is it me or is it cold in here all of a sudden?" Janet asked of Lisa while rubbing her arms with her hands.

"I think it's just you for the time be-," Lisa responds before stopping mid-sentence.

Lisa suddenly feels that cold chill up her spine that Janet just spoke of with the hair on the back of her neck begins to rise.

"I think it's time to go. I just felt that coldness you mentioned a second ago. Something definitely is not right about this place. I think it's time to go," Lisa says with a shaky tone to her voice.

Janet looks back at the painting to notice something strange. "Is it me or is that painting smiling at us now?" Janet asked while getting scared.

"I think it's time to get back to the guys now."

"Couldn't agree more Lisa," Janet says while backing out of the room. "Let's get back to the guys."

The two suddenly hear a strange noise in the den from the direction of the painting and just begin running back to where they last saw Marcus and William. Just as Lisa is clearing the door to the den, she trips over something on the floor causing a thick cloud of dust to mushroom into the air above her.

"Are you ok?" Janet asked while coming back to check on Lisa.

"Yeah, I think I am," Lisa responds while checking herself out for injuries.

"What did you trip over?"

The two start to shine their flashlights in the direction where Lisa tripped, only to see a big cloud of dust particles reflecting in the beams of the flashlights. As the dust begins to resettle, they are able to see that Lisa tripped over a dismembered leg that appears rats have chewed cleanly through to the bone. The two women look at each other than back down at the severed leg before taking off screaming down the hall towards Marcus and William.

"AHH!" Lisa screams as she begins running down the hall.

"I'm right behind you!" Janet screams.

The two run so fast up the hallway back towards Marcus and William that Janet nearly crashes into Marcus as he is heading towards them to see why the two women are screaming.

"Whoa!" Marcus puts his hands up just before Janet barrels into him at full speed. "What's going on?"

"L-L-Leg…" Janet tries to finish her sentence but is so out of breath and scared. "I-It was a severed leg in the hallway and s-something creepy happened in the other room."

"A leg?" Marcus asked. "What about the leg?"

"It was bitten clean through with no body attached to it," Lisa says while hunched over with her hands on her thighs while huffing and puffing for air.

"You two are ok though, right?" Marcus asked."

"We are," Lisa replied still sounding a little shaky. "I want to go home…NOW!"

"HEY! I think I found something over here!" William yells out from another room next to where Marcus was standing with Lisa and Janet.

"We'll be right there," Marcus yells back.

The three gather themselves and walk over to where William was yelling. Noticeably still shaken from the incident in the hallway, Lisa is looking back and forth in a nervous manner while shining her flashlight all over the tiny room from whence William was yelling.

The room they are all standing in is no bigger than a glorified broom closet. Just wide enough for Marcus to spread his arms out wide with his fingertips just touching both sides of the walls. Dusty cobwebs hang from the corners of the low-lying ceiling like dust-covered chandeliers while the old paint, chips and flakes off the walls. With each movement in the congested room they make, the more dust fills the stale tasting atmosphere.

"Hurry up and open that door. Some of us are dying back here," Janet says while trying not to sneeze through her mask.

"I still find it creepy how no one else is here, was here, or demolished this house," Lisa says from the back of the group.

"Somebody is paying for the land. We all know as long as the city is getting there money, they could care less about an abandoned property," Marcus responds. "As for the bums who ventured, I guess you saw that the rats got them."

As Marcus is responding to Lisa and Janet, William is busy trying to get the door open trying to break down the door. Checking the door for any sharp objects sticking out before laying his shoulder into the door. “This is one strong wooden door for it to be so old and decayed,” he added.

“Or you’re just a weak little mouse,” Janet sarcastically says.

That must have gotten under William’s skin because he let out one loud scream of rage before proceeding to kick the door in just above the doorknob. “Who’s the weakling now?” He turns back looking at Janet and smiling.

A rush of cold stale air rushes into the tiny room in which they are standing once the door has been kicked open.

“You still are,” Janet replies. “You kicked in a centuries old door.”

“Now that stinks,” Lisa says referring to the air that rushed into the room.

Everyone just starts laughing at the situation before Lisa intervenes about getting this over with so she can just get out of the house and back home.

“Can we just hurry up and get this done so we can get out of here?” Lisa questions the group.

“Ok, ok, ok. Let’s hurry this up and get out of this place. It’s starting to really creep me out,” Janet says.

“So who wants to go first?” Marcus asked while shining his light on every one.

William sticks his flashlight just inside of the doorway to

get some light on the entrance of the basement. Like shooting a beam of light into space, there is nothing but a dark void with nothing for the light to reflect off in the process.

It is not until William points his flashlight down towards the floor that he is able to see a stone style landing leading down into the darkness along the side of the wall. There is also a broken; in several spots, decayed wooden railing running the length of the steps that William can see with his flashlight. By the looks of the railing, it is liable to break apart at thc slightest of any weight-baring object.

“Who wants to go first?” Marcus inquires. “This mask sucks after filtering out stinking stale air.”

“We don’t even know how far down these steps go,” said Lisa. “Let alone if they actually make it all the way to the bottom.”

“I got this,” said Marcus as he reaches down into his pocket and pulls out a quarter. “Let’s see just how far down these steps really go. If we don’t hear anything, we’ll just throw William down there and he can tell us.”

“Ha…ha. Real funny.”

Marcus squeezes past William to get to the inside of the doorway before throwing his quarter down the steps. He flips the quarter into the air as if he is a referee doing the coin toss before the start of a football game. After about three seconds of flipping through the air, the first sound of the quarter hitting the stone stairs echoes. Than another second later silence fills the stale basement air.

Silence fills the small closet sized room just outside of the basement door with the four friends just staring at one another with the flashlights pointed up at the ceiling before Janet decides to break the silence with a sarcastic remark.

"Can we throw William down the steps now? I'm asking for a friend."

"I'll go myself. I don't need your help getting down there any faster, thank you very much."

Chapter Eight

Down Into The Darkness

William is the first to step onto the stone landing that will begin his downward descent into the darkness of the eerie and unknown basement atmosphere. He places his right hand on the cold and damp wall as a guide before something ran across the tips of his fingers causing him to jump back nearly falling back up the steps, sending the beam of his flashlight swirling into the air.

The other three jump back in fear as they are standing in the doorway of the basement after hearing William yell out and they see his flashlight going crazy.

"Are you ok?" Lisa yells down to William while shining her light down on him.

"I'm fine. Just slipped a little bit on the steps. Come on down so we can find this money. The steps aren't crumbling so we should be good. Just don't touch the walls. Pretty sure it's something on them."

The three remaining friends walk out onto the landing one at a time with Marcus leading the way with Lisa and Janet in tow behind him. They shine their flashlights down the stairs and along the wall to make sure not to miss anything.

The walls are cold, damp and chipping from the wet atmosphere with cobwebs hanging from almost every inch leading down into the basement.

Once Marcus is down three steps, there is no wall to the left of the stairs and no railing to hold on to while walking down the stone steps.

"Everyone watch where you step. How you doing down there Will?" Janet asked while trying not to touch the slimy cobweb filled walls on her way down.

"I'm fine. Just another walk in the park," he replies to Janet. "It's very slippery down where I am. Hopefully I'm close to the bottom. Can't see anything even with this flashlight."

Lisa being as scared as she is as she walks down the steps can be heard mumbling words to herself as she slowly walks down the steps behind Marcus.

"What are you saying Lisa? You good?" Marcus stops on the steps to ask.

Just as Lisa is preparing to answer Marcus' question, she lets out a loud scream with her flashlight going all over the place.

"Get it off of me! Get it off! It's on my arm!" She screams out while jumping up and down while brushing off her arms and chest.

Janet, who is just a few steps above Lisa, quickly stops in her tracks and proceeds to scan Lisa with her flashlight. It is hard for Janet to get a good view of Lisa's body due to how she is reacting to the possibility of something crawling on her arms.

"Keep still Lisa so I can check you out," Janet says to a shaking and frantic Lisa.

After walking down the steps leading deeper into the house, with several near slips, and what seemed like minutes of walking deeper into the depths, William hits the bottom of the stone steps only to hear a small splashing sound as his right sneaker touched down onto the basement floor.

"Aww man! The basement floor is flooded!" William yells out.

"What's going on up there?" William yells from the bottom of the steps.

Marcus runs back up the steps to help Janet calm down Lisa while making sure he does not slip on the damp steps.

"I felt it on me. It was something crawling on my right arm. I'm not crazy," Lisa replied while looking herself up and down with her flashlight. "I knew I should have went home."

"It's ok Lisa. We got you. You are going to be fine. There is nothing crawling on you. Do you still feel something crawling on you?" asked Marcus.

Janet proceeds to hug Lisa after checking her several times from top to bottom for anything crawling on her clothes.

Marcus looks at the wall where Lisa and Janet are standing to notice that something is waving in the low wind current. He shines his light at an angle to the wall to see a clumped but thin layer of cobwebs waving from the wall and extending to the area where Lisa was standing when she felt something crawling on her arm.

"Everything will be ok. Your arm just brushed up against some cobwebs that were stuck to the wall. No need to worry."

"Ok. Can we just get to the basement and get out of here?"

William, who is still down at the bottom of the steps, is scanning the area with his flashlight as he sees the other three are finally making their way down to him.

"This place is creepy," William says just under his breath

as he continues to look around the basement.

At the bottom of the damp cold steps, leads to an area no bigger than a small ten by ten bedroom. There are four stone pillars rising from the floor to the ceiling in the four corners of the room. The air in this tiny space is even denser with a thick smell of mildew. It does not help that there is a half inch of water on the floor throughout the basement.

A moist green mossy type substance covers the walls and the pillars that appears to thrive in this damp environment. As William scans the enclosure with his flashlight, he sees shadows of things crawling away from his light into giants cracks in the walls.

"Oh man, this place is a mess. What were we thinking coming here?" Marcus says while walking over next to William.

William turned around slowly to face Marcus with his flashlight just under his chin.

"You came for the adventure and to dispel an urban legend," he says with a creepy tone to his voice.

Janet and Lisa walk over to join William and Marcus near the back wall of the basement.

"And you came because you think you can get rich with your greedy self," Janet says towards William.

"I try."

Lisa is standing behind everyone looking up at the ceiling while brushing the gnats that continue to fly around the basement and landing on her arms and legs.

"Can we hurry up and get out of here?" Lisa asked. "Who forgot to bring bug spray? I hate bugs!"

The four of them are together in the dark, damp spider and bug filled basement wondering what to do next while continuing to swat away the thoughts of something crawling on their body

"So now what?" Janet asked. "Don't tell me we came down here for nothing just to sit in a waterlogged bug infested basement."

Just as Janet finishes her statement, the four hear a low creaking noise before it starts getting louder and louder. Suddenly, a loud slamming noise echoes throughout the basement. The door leading upstairs slams shut locking the foursome in complete darkness in the basement before hearing a low wailing voice fills the room sending chills down their spine.

"You…are…doomed f-for eternitttty," says an unknown eerie ghostly voice.

The four jump in fear before huddling together back to back with their flashlights scanning all over the basement before they mysteriously start flickering before turning off while a cold chill sweeps into the room surrounding them.

An eerie white and bluish glow illuminates the whole basement, that forms by the stairs leading back upstairs, before a skeletal hand starts to form while pointing at them that moves closer to the group. The eerie ghostly finger is within five feet of the friends before it stops in front of William just pointing at him. As fast as the eerie ghostly glow appears, it turns to mist and goes through the cobblestone wall to the right of the group but not before leaving a message for the four.

"Beeee goonne!"

After the sudden and unexpected visit by the unknown ghost, the four friends are scared and unable to speak. Their flashlights flicker several times before powering on again. The cold atmosphere returns to room temperature as if the ghost never appeared leaving the four friends scared and shaken.

A dim bluish trail, left behind as the apparition disappears into the wall began to illuminate a small circular hole that was brightly visible without a flashlight. The four friends are staring at each other in confusion as to what just occurred.

William steadies himself and begins to walk over to the wall in which the apparition disappeared; however, not before Lisa grabs his arm in a manner of not wanting him to get any closer. He merely looks back at her with a smile while continuing to walk towards the glowing section of the wall.

Marcus walks up next to William as they just stare at the glowing hole in the wall.

"Well, you asked what's next Janet. Well here's your answer," said Marcus.

The four gather around the cobblestone hole in the wall, which is no bigger than the size of a half dollar coin, which is glowing a dim blue.

"So what are we suppose to do now?" asked Lisa.

"Stick your finger in there Janet and see what happens. Can't mess up your nails any more than what they already are now," said William with a sarcastic tone.

Janet shoots a glaring look at William before responding to his sarcasm.

"Hell no! I'm not sticking my finger in there just to get bit by some blood sucking spider or bug so my hand can swell up to the size of a balloon. You put your finger in there."

"Stick your finger in there William. You're the one who wanted to be here. Hurry up because I don't like being around all these spiders and bugs," Lisa chimed in on the conversation.

"Fine. I'm surrounded by a bunch of punks," says William as he walks closer to the glowing hole in the wall while brushing away the bugs and cobwebs.

As he goes to slide his finger into the glowing hole in the cobblestone wall, he hesitates and instead tries to fit his flashlight into the tiny hole then backs away.

"How do we even know it's a button in this hole and not some poisonous creature in there waiting to bite my finger off?

"We don't. Now stick your finger in there so I can get a good laugh if something does bite you," Janet sarcastically says to William.

Lisa and Marcus are just sitting back with their flashlights pointed in William's direction waiting anxiously to see what happens when and if he sticks his finger into the hole in the wall.

"Come on Mr. Big Talker. Get your ass in gear," Janet taunts William.

William takes a few steps away from the wall with water splashing around him with each step as he attempts to hype himself up for the task at hand. Mumbling to himself about how he's not afraid of anything and he can do this.

Walking back over to the hole in the cobblestone wall, William proceeds to wipe away the bugs crawling over the opening upon sticking his finger inside. He did not even slide his finger in past the first inch before pulling it back out quickly and letting out a loud scream.

Lisa lets out a loud scream and starts freaking out while Janet and Marcus jump back while keeping their flashlights on William.

"MY FINGER!" William screams out while bending over and tucking his finger into his stomach.

"Oh my goodness baby!" Lisa runs over to William.

Marcus and Janet are just looking at it each in shock after what they just witnessed.

William leans up against the wall next to the opening, not caring about the cobwebs and bugs crawling along the surface, with Lisa standing next to him sounds frantic.

"Let me see your finger," said Lisa.

William just starts laughing while walking back over to the hole in the wall. Still hiding his finger from Lisa as she continues to try to see how bad of an injury he has.

"This is too easy," William says while laughing. "There is nothing wrong with my finger…see." As he shows everyone his perfectly intact uninjured finger.

Lisa walks over to William and smacks him in the back of his head.

"What you do that for?" said William as he starts rubbing the back of his head.

"Just get me out of here!" Lisa demands.

Mumbling something under his breath before proceeding to place his finger into the hole in the hopes that there is actually a button there to open a secret passage so they can continue the hunt for the hidden pirate treasure.

William can feel the tiny bugs crawling over his finger as he slides it deeper into the damp and slimy hole before hitting a diamond shaped object at the back of the opening.

"I just hit something."

Everyone's flashlights focus on William.

"So push it. What are you waiting for?" questioned Janet.

"If my finger gets chopped off, I'm blaming all of you."

"Whatever."

William proceeds to push into the diamond shaped object at the back of the finger-sized opening and quickly pulls his finger out before anything can happen to him.

"Still have your finger I see," said Marcus in a sarcastic tone. "Now what?"

"No idea."

A low mumble begins to erupt before growing louder while the floor starts to tremble with vibration.

"You just had to ask, didn't you?" yelled Janet as she's trying to brace herself against the back wall.

The wall where the mysteriously glowing hole in the wall begins to rise, slowly dimming it's glow. The gang shine their flashlights at the slowly rising entrance that leads into another dark room.

After several seconds of the door rising, it comes to a complete stop along with the room no longer shaking.

"What the hell died in there?" says Marcus as the air rushes out from behind the once closed hidden door.

Everyone rushes over to the now open enclosure to see what could possibly be hiding on the other side. Just inside the opening, they can see a ledge that extends about fifteen feet before their flashlight beams are absorbed by the darkness. To the right and left of the opening, there are no visible walls with nothing but pure darkness.

"Probably some rats. Maybe even those missing homeless people that came in here," says William.

"Nope, I'm not going in there," Janet says loudly.

"Oh yes you are. You're already down here," Marcus replies. "So who wants to go first?"

William sticks his head into the opening with his flashlight before stepping out onto the stone ledge. He notices that the ledge is wide enough for everyone to stand on if standing next to each other. He proceeds to cautiously walk out as far as his flashlight shines in front of him.

"Better watch your step homie. You don't know what's out there," Marcus shouts out to William.

"I got this!"

William walks about fourteen feet from the entrance when his flashlight illuminates a skinny rope bridge with boards as the pathway.

"Come on over. I found a rope bridge with some old wooden boards for a flooring," shouts William to the rest of the crew.

The three walk over to where William is standing huddled

together as to not fall off thc side of the landing. There is nothing but complete darkness except for the illumination of their flashlights. The air has an odor of mildew, dust, and a backed up sewer line filling the atmosphere, making it hard to breathe even with their dust mask covering their faces. The path is littered with dead bug carcasses that crunch with each step they take along with fallen cobwebs floating into the air.

"A bridge? How big is this damn place?" Lisa asked.

"So…who wants to go first?" asked Marcus as he just throws that question out there.

Janet walks over to the rope bridge and tugs on the suspension then shakes the ropes up and down a few times. With each shake, dust jumps up and down off the ropes as the plank flooring creeks.

"Seems pretty stable to me," says Janet in a sarcastic tone. "Certified death trap here that's for sure."

"It can't be that bad. Not like many people walked on this lately," replied William as he gently presses his foot on the first plank of the bridge flooring while applying a little bit of weight. "See, no problem whatso--,"

As he applies a little more pressure to the board, it can be heard beginning to creek and possibly snap.

"You were saying?" Janet questions William.

"Well, just don't step on that first one and we'll be all good," he says while pointing down at the first plank.

"I wonder how far this thing goes across," says Lisa while looking over the edge. "Hell, let along how deep is the drop."

Marcus pulls out another quarter that he intended to use for the arcade before the meet up and flips it over the edge to listen for the sound of hitting the bottom.

Within three seconds of flipping the quarter over the edge, the group of four hear a plopping noise of what sounds as if the quarter landed in a pool of water.

"I would hate to know what's floating down there," Marcus says while backing away from the edge. "Guess, I won't be getting that quarter back now."

Before anyone can turn around and recover from the newest discovery of this mysterious house, William has already gingerly walking across the bridge and already four steps away from his friends.

With each steps William takes, he lightly applies some pressure to test the sturdiness of the next plank on the bridge. The planks may be old, damp, and splintered but they are strong enough to hold the weight of William without breaking.

"Come on people. What are you waiting for? Just take your time and you'll be fine. Just don't look down," he says while laughing.

"Not funny," Lisa blurts out.

"Just come on."

The remaining three line up with Janet first followed by Lisa with Marcus pulling up the rear. Each giving the other a few steps before following behind in order to cross the shaky structure.

When everyone is just about halfway across the bridge, an extremely cold breeze blows from one end to the other. Everyone stops dead in their tracks and just stands there shaking.

"Damn that was cold. Please tell me the rest of you felt that?" shouted William.

"Why can I see my breath?" asked Lisa as she holds her hand in front of her mouth.

"Where did that breeze come from?" asked Janet.

No sooner than Janet finishes her question to everyone, an apparition of the same familiar bluish hue appears on the left side of the group seemingly from out of nowhere.

"Stay out of my chamber! Those that seek the treasures of Red Point the Pirate will perish upon its touch!" in an eerie and scary voice shouts the apparition.

Just as fast as the apparition appears, it quickly disappears after delivering his eerie and creepy warning message. The atmosphere returns to how it was before the apparition appeared.

"Well, that was interesting," Marcus says in a calm voice while he's trying to cover up how fast his heart is racing after the encounter.

"If that's how you want to put what just happened…sure," replied Janet in a not so calm voice.

After everyone regains their composure, they quickly make their way off the bridge to the other side, which continues into a dark damp corridor deeper into the basement.

On the other side of the bridge is also a cobblestone type flooring that is somewhat slippery due to the damp condition in this lower half of the house. A strong odor of mildew lingers throughout the air along with a constant dripping of water can be heard from an unknown and unseen source.

"I was not expecting to see that. Not in the least bit. Who the hell was that?" Janet says while trying to calm down from the ghostly encounter.

"I have no clue," Marcus said to Janet while his hands are on his knees as he's bending over. "He or it…whatever didn't look like a pirate. That ghost looked a little scruffy. Probably one of those bums that disappeared."

A few minutes pass after everyone attempts to regain their wits about themselves before proceeding down the dark damp hallway leading deeper into the house's unknown basement. A constant dripping can be heard echoing throughout the lower levels of the house as it plops onto the cobblestone style flooring.

The four slowly advance deeper into the hallway after being scared half to death on the rope bridge by their ghostly encounter with flashlights scanning every corner of the tight damp corridor. Lisa stops and turns her flashlight back to the rope bridge, as she cannot believe that she just walked across the broken and dilapidated planks and survived. Unknown to her, a spider began descending down towards her left shoulder as she is standing there in amazement about the bridge.

"You coming with us or not, Lisa?" William yells back.

Hearing William call her name snaps Lisa out of the trance of disbelief she has been in for the past several seconds.

"W-What? Yeah, I'm on my way," Lisa responds back yelling to William. Just as she takes two steps from her previous location, the spider lands harmlessly on to the floor and crawls away. The group stops advancing and waits for Lisa to catch up with them before proceeding.

"Come on slow poke. You believe in haunted houses now

Lisa?" William asked of her as she approaches the group of three waiting on her to catch up.

"After today, I wouldn't be surprised if I saw raptors running around the city once we get out of this place," Lisa replied.

The walls of the corridor are slowly closing in the deeper they go, and are just wide enough for the four friends to walk two by two with a door standing between them and whatever is on the other side at the very end of the corridor.

"Why is this hallway getting tighter? I can damn near touch both sides of the walls. Something isn't right here," Janet says while shining her flashlight around herself. "Even the ceiling is getting lower. What is going on here?"

"You're right. I didn't even notice the ceiling," Marcus replied.

"The hell with that. It's time to-," William mutters out before an interruption by Lisa occurred.

"Look! There's a door!"

The door is barely visible from the distance at which the four friends are standing. Upon moving closer, they can see that it is an old withered wooden door with rusted metal plating along the top, bottom and middle. Not having a traditional door handle, there hangs an old sturdy Viking style metal ring in its place.

"Push or pull?" Marcus breaks the silence.

"Old door like that looks like a pull," Janet replies.

"So who wants to pull the door to the hidden riches of the world?"

William steps up to the door, taking ahold of the large

metal ring, and begins to pull out towards the right of the entrance but with no luck. The large withered and metal door does not budge an inch with William pulling as hard as he can.

"Oh, I see everyone just seeing me struggle and will just stand there and not help a brother out."

"Yeah…pretty much," Janet replies sarcastically.

"Whatever!"

Marcus walks over to the left side of William and grabs ahold of the metal ring with both hands tight. The two brace themselves to pull on the heavy wooden door. The two agree to pull the handle at the count of three.

"This door feels heavy as hell," says Marcus as he gives the door a little tug before getting ready with William to try to pull it open.

"You ready?"

"Let's do this!"

The two of them brace themselves for the heavy pull on the count of three while Janet and Lisa continue to look around the door and the walls around them.

The two guys pull with all of their might as they dig their feet onto the slippery cobblestone flooring for better traction but to no avail. Suddenly, the door gives a little as dust and debris start falling from the top of the frame.

"Are you even pulling William? Feels like I'm about to give myself a hernia."

"Stop being a baby!"

The door gives a little before jamming and locking itself into place causing William and Marcus to lose their grip and fall onto the damp cobblestone floor.

"What happened?" Janet asked as she runs over to help Marcus and William up off the floor with Lisa right beside her.

Wiping the dirt and drying his hands off on his shorts. "The door felt like it just jammed and locked up. Don't know what happened," Marcus replied. "Has to be a button or something to release the door."

"That ghost probably locked it from the other side," William says sarcastically as he kicks the door. "Stupid door."

"I haven't seen anything that would even look like a release for the door," said Lisa.

The four start searching for anything that can possibly resemble a release button or lever for the now locked wooden door that stands between them and a possibility of becoming rich.

Marcus and William search from the left side of the door and along the adjacent wall while Lisa and Janet search on the opposite side.

"What exactly are we looking for?" Lisa asked with a questionable tone to her voice as she moved her flashlight up and down the damp slimy walls.

"Anything that would or could be pressed, pulled, lifted up or down would be my guess. And something that seems out of place," Marcus responded.

Not even seconds pass before Janet signals to the group that she may have found something along the right side of the lower end of the wall just seven feet away from the old wooden door.

“I think I found something.”

The three rush over to where Janet is kneeling.

“What did you find?” William asks with excitement.

“I don’t know but I will say it’s not normal. I only saw it because I shined my flashlight over the spot and it lit up. Other than that, I could not see it in this darkness. Watch.”

Janet moves her flashlight back and forth over the spot she pointed out to everyone to show the shimmer that appears once hit with the flashlight beam. As she moves the flashlight away from the location of the shimmer, the darkness once again engulfs the area.

“Kind of has that blue glow like the other one,” said Lisa as Janet shines her flashlight back over the area.

“You found it, you pull it,” said Marcus as he leans on Janet’s shoulder.

Janet shines her flashlight over the section of the wall containing the lever. At this time, everyone is shaking with the anticipation as to what is going to happen next. This lever, covered in dirt-entangled cobwebs has a hole just wide enough to reach inside to pull the lever forward to what they hope will release the door lock allowing them to enter.

“You know I hate spiders, right?” said Janet as she hesitates to reach inside of the hole.

“Yeah yeah. Quit stalling. It’s time to get paid up in here,” said William in a sarcastic tone. “I already stuck my hand inside and released a door. It’s your turn now.”

Janet kneels down to the same level as the lever with her

right hand extending but shaking so nervously. As she reaches for the lever, a long millipede comes crawling out the hole and up the wall, causing Janet to jump back in fear and nearly drop her flashlight.

Everyone takes a step back as Janet jumps away from the hole, falling back on her hands and butt to the slimy wet floor of the dark hallway after seeing the giant millipede crawl out and up the right of the wall.

"Eww! Feels like I landed in a slime pit," said Janet as she is getting up and wiping her hands onto her shorts.
"Time…to…go. Like…NOW!"

"Move out of the way," William said as he slides past Marcus towards the hole containing the lever.

As William walks over to the hole shining his light on the location of the lever. He calmly slides his hand into the illuminated hole grasping the lever. Mentally blocking out the feet of the various insects crawling all over his hand as he pulls the lever towards him until they hear a loud clicking sound and it no longer moves.

William pulls his hand out quickly as he brushing the bugs off his hand and forearm. "Stupid bugs!"

"It clicked so let's see what's behind the magic door," said Marcus well walking back over to the door. "Give me a hand with this ring William."

The two take ahold of the ring and begin pulling. To the surprise of the group, the door slowly screeches open revealing a pitch-black room on the other side.

Chapter Nine

The Other Side

As the door finally sits open after the ordeal of pulling the lever has passed, the crew of four curious and somewhat mentally shaken friends stare into the darkness of the unknown.

The room appears to be the size of an average living room. About 16' x 20', covered in nearly floor to ceiling dust. At the center of the room sits a large round table that looks to seat six to eight people but there are no chairs, but instead covered by a large dust colored tarp type material.

On top of said table, sits a rather creepy and somewhat out of place cracked rotting skull. In which when the four friends illuminate the skull, all that can be seen are what appears to be sparkling lights like that of a starry night sky reflecting back at them.

"Now that's that is done. Who wants to go first?" said Marcus.

"Janet should go first since she couldn't even pull the lever," said William while letting off a smirk.

Janet gives William the look of shooting daggers through her eyes at him.

"I'm just messing with you J. No need for hostilities. We all want to get paid."

"Funny."

The four are just standing around the door peering inside with their flashlights but can see no farther than the table in the middle of the room.

"So who is going in first?" asked Marcus.

"I'll go fir-," William starts to say before a cold wind blasts out of the room in which they are standing in front of.

The four friends are just standing in the doorway stiff as a board after the blast of cold air came shooting out of the room. Along with the cold wind came a stench of mold and dust filling the long skinny pathway.

"Oh man! Can this air quality get any worse?" Lisa blurted out while covering her mask with her hand.

"Would you prefer a dead decaying body? I'm sure we can find one of those for you."

"Shut up Will!"

William now standing in the doorway, running his flashlight around the frame of the door and a few feet into the room's dark floor. Slowly stepping into the room, cautious with each step as he nervously moves his flashlight quickly from left to right from floor to ceiling and wall-to-wall.

"You see anything?" asked Lisa from outside of the room.

"Nothing yet. Come on in." replied William as he's about halfway into the room.

The remaining three slowly slip into the room with Janet leading the pack slowly, followed by Lisa with Marcus pulling up the rear.

Once inside, they huddle around the table with Janet and

Marcus on nine o'clock side with William and Lisa on the three o'clock with their flashlights solely focused on the skull in the middle of the table.

"Well. Now we know why the skull was sparkling," said Marcus as he is looking down while watching small beetle like insects run inside and out of the decrepit skull.

"Man! I thought I was about to be rich," said William as he stepped away from the trouble in frustration.

"What happened to WE?" Janet quickly fired back.

"Well...um...yeah. It would be WE but I was speaking for myself in terms of spending *MY* portion of the money."

"Whatever."

The room is slightly colder than it was coming down into the dark damp basement and over the rickety bridge. Old cobwebs hang from the ceiling in large clumps that sway from side to side from the stale moldy draft air even more so with the large door now being open. The walls, covered in a moldy type slime and dirt have various bugs scurrying along the wall.

"This is freaky," said Lisa as she begins to walk around the room while shining her flashlight around.

"Welcome to a dead end guys," said Janet.

William starts walking angrily back towards the table from the right side of the room.

"I did not come all this way for nothing. I'm getting paid one way or another!" yelled William as he proceeds to swing his flashlight at the skull on the table like a baseball bat, sending the skull flying across the room. Sending the bugs on the table into a scattering frenzy.

The skull smashes into the wall not far from where Marcus was standing.

"Well aren't we bold now," Janet said while looking at William. "Feel better now?"

"No!"

No sooner than William finishes his reply that the room begins violently shaking as if an earthquake just hit and they were at ground zero.

"What the hell did you do William?" shouted Lisa

"Nothing!"

Dirt and debris start falling off the ceiling as the room continues to shake violently.

"This is your fault William. If you didn't smash that skull," said Marcus.

"No it's not."

Suddenly the floor begins to split down the middle of the room from the edge of the door, shooting straight under the table to the back of the room causing the table to buckle to the right due to the crack opening wider. The four friends brace themselves up against the walls on opposite sides of the enlarging crack.

"This is your damn fault William!" yelled Janet from across the room.

"No it's not!"

In that instant, the room suddenly stops shaking as the table sticks out from the crack in the floor.

"Is it over?" asked Janet.

"Let's hope so," responded Marcus.

"So now what?" Lisa asked in a scared yet questionable tone.

No sooner than Lisa finishes her sentence, Marcus spots a board rising up from the floor, just in front of the door in which they entered with a razor tipped arrow protruding from the middle.

"Hit the floor!" Marcus yells out to everyone.

Lisa yanked William not realizing what is going on, down to the floor, just before an arrow zips over the top of his head.

Lisa shines her light behind her where the arrow just flew over her head. "Damn! That could have been us pinned to the wall."

"Filled with pinholes with feathers sticking out," added Janet.

"Then try drinking something like Tom just waiting and watching for the liquid to sprinkle out," said Marcus.

"Now that would be kind of funny."

"You have a sick sense of humor Janet," Marcus says while having a weird look on his face.

Lisa is now sounding even more scared after the recent events while starting to pick herself up off the floor.

"We almost died and yall cracking jokes. Yall have some serious deep rooted issues going on in your lives."

"Your point?" Marcus asked.

"Don't talk to me anymore."

"Ok," Marcus says in a sarcastic tone.

The four all get up off the floor while dusting themselves off and huddling up around the giant crack in the floor in which the table now sinks into.

"This is beyond creepy now. All this and no gold. I don't even want to know what's going to happen next." Janet says while sounding frustrated.

"I know that damn gold better be in this basement somewhere!" William says.

William now looking at the shattered skull that lies scattered all over the floor in several big pieces. "Look at this! All this trouble for nothing."

Suddenly a door at the back of the room, directly across from the entrance in which they entered, slowly begins to break the cobblestone wall making the tiny room shake in the process. Dropping more dirt, dust and debris from the ceiling onto the group of four.

"What the hell is going on?"

"This is your "what now" answer, Janet." Marcus replied. "I hope you're enjoying the answer to your question."

They are quick to shine their flashlights on the slowly opening stone door, as they do not know what to expect from this new occurrence. What appeared to be a solid stone back wall begins to push into another room a few inches before grinding slowly to the right along the wall.

"What the hell now?" Lisa asked in a scared but questionable tone.

"I have no idea." Janet replied.

"This grinding sound is worse than nails on a chalkboard," Marcus says. "This things needs to hurry up asap."

After several minutes, the slow grinding cobblestone wall is completely open, unveiling a room of complete darkness on the other side.

"Peep that. I see something reflecting off the light," said William.

"What?" questioned Lisa.

"I don't know. Go look Marcus."

"You go! You're the one with gold fever," Marcus quickly responded.

Now that the door is completely open, the four huddle around the entrance while shining their flashlights onto the reflective objects off in the distance. The room is so dark it is hard for them to see anything past the range of their flashlights.

"Someone needs to go peek inside," Janet says while sounding demanding.

"Who do you think you are giving orders?" William fires back quickly.

"Yo momma!"

"Whatever. I'm calling first dibs on the gold."

All you hear is a sigh from Lisa in the background.

"Really?"

William is the first to stick his flashlight in the door to test for booby traps before going completely inside. He cautiously proceeds to poke his head inside while looking left and right slowly scanning across the room from floor to ceiling. As he finally steps foot into the room, something catches his eye off to his right causing him to jump back.

"What's going on in there?" Lisa asked.

Sounding nervous about what he just saw, William has his right hand on his chest trying to shake the nerves off.

"Wow. That scared the hell out of me. It's a candle that just lit."

"A candle?" Marcus says sounding surprised.

Just as Marcus finishes his question, the secret room suddenly starts brightening up as candles start to flicker to life as if someone was running around the room lighting each one quickly.

"Now that is just freaky," said Janet.

As the room becomes brighter and brighter with each candle lighting, the reflective object that the friends saw is slowly coming into focus.

"Oh shit! It's the gold! A whole room full of chests just waiting for me to plunder!"

William's eye get wide and the biggest grin appears on his face as he starts rubbing his hands together.

"Now that's a lot of gold," said Marcus.

"It's all mines. Mines! Mines! Mines!"

The three friends are looking at William with the expression on their faces of someone who just lost their mind.

In that same instance, William takes off running deeper into the secret room. Just as fast as he ran inside, he is quickly stopping in his tracks.

"Wait!" Lisa yells out.

The three run in behind him to see why he stopped so abruptly, only to find out that a spider the size of a fist dropped down on top of the gold.

"Now that's a big spider," said Janet.

"I'm out of here!" Lisa says while backing away slowly.

The spider is now crawling down off the gold pile and is quickly scurrying over towards the four friends.

"Kill that thing! Step on it!" Janet yelled out.

"Won't be me!"

"Not surprised William. Is that thing getting bigger?" Marcus says while backing up.

The spider, nearly three times its original size with wavy red stripes on its eight furry legs, a bright red spot on the middle of its back, and two big fangs sticking out of its mouth makes its way closer and closer to the friends of four.

Nearly halfway back into the previous room in which they just came from, they are running out of real estate as the board full of arrows is now blocking their main escape from the ever-growing spider.

"W-what are we going to do? That thing is coming through

the door and is just as big as the door," said Lisa as she shaking and scared.

"Go pet it on the head and tell it what a good spider it is Janet."

"You first William."

The four friends try to go two by two on opposite sides of the room so they are not together, in case the spider was to attack them directly.

"What are we doing people? Remind me to stay home next time you decide to go haunted house creeping," Lisa says frantically.

"If we live that long," Marcus replied.

Looking around trying to find anything that can be used as a possible weapon; Janet attempts to pull one of the arrows out of the wall.

"What are you doing woman?" Marcus asked.

"Trying to get a few of these arrows out of the wall. I need something to use as a weapon."

"Like that will help. It's as big as I am."

"Then it's not that big at all."

"This is no time to be cracking jokes."

The spider, now the size of a baby elephant, is turning left and right as it looks at the two group of friends along the walls of the dark room.

"Lisa...William! Look for arrows!" Janet yelled across the

room.

The spider is just watching the four slowly move along the wall as it sits just above the giant crack in the middle of the floor cleaning its mouth.

William not paying attention to where he walking backs right into an arrow that is protruding out of the wall, jabbing him in the back of his right shoulder.

"Son of a b-," William yells out.

The spider quickly turns his attention to William who is pulling an arrow out of the wall after it scratched the back of his shoulder.

"Now what?" As he waves the long tipped arrow in the direction of the spider. "He's looking at me."

"So look back at it," said Marcus.

"What the hell kind of crap is that to say?"

"Sue me!"

"I will!"

Everyone slowly reaches and grabs an arrow anywhere they can find one and slowly start spreading out to break the spider's focus so they can plan a form of escape or attack.

"I want to go home," Lisa quietly cried out as she clutches the arrow tightly in her hands.

"We'll get home," Janet says reassuring Lisa.

Marcus takes one-step to his right as slowly as he could without being noticed by the spider who suddenly shifted his focus from William over to Marcus. The spider is still cleaning his mandibles while it bounces up and down as if it is preparing to strike one of the four friends.

"Happy now? The ugly arachnid is looking at me now," Marcus yelled over to William.

"Very."

"Bastard!"

The spider slowly starts making its way over to Marcus before Janet yells out trying to get its attention on her.

"What are you doing woman?" Marcus asked.

"I don't know."

Just as the giant spider turns to direct its attention to Janet, William raises his hand and runs toward the spider, arrow tightly gripped in his right hand, while letting out what would considered a battle cry.

"Die spider!" said William while leaping into the air towards his target.

"No William!" Janet yells out.

As fast as William leaps into the air, the spider is just as fast encasing him in a thick web that hits William with such force that he slams back into the wall. The three friends are in complete shock as to what just happened.

"Well…that explains the bones and skulls scattered all over the place," said Marcus in a sarcastic icebreaker tone.

"U-ugh! Shut up and get me out of here!" shouted William who briefly had the wind knocked out of him after slamming into the wall.

The spider quickly turns its whole body towards a now web covered William before Janet once again intervenes and draws the spider's attention back on her.

"*You* are crazy, woman," said Marcus as he watched Janet continuing to wave her arms and yell at the spider. "Do spiders even have ears?"

Lisa, standing just a few feet away from a web covered William, is paralyzed with fear as to what has just unfolded. She is staring, as William is yelling something but cannot hear anything due to her being so scared. Her heart is racing, as she is standing straight up against the wall clutching the broken arrow tightly in her left hand.

"LISA! LISA! Snap out of it woman! Get me out of here!" William yells at the top of his lungs.

After several moments of being in a trance like state, Lisa finally snaps back to reality to hear William's voice calling out to her and seeing Janet waving her arms at the spider.

"W-What?"

"Get me out of here!" as William called out again to a stunned Lisa.

Lisa slowly starts sliding over towards William to cut him out of his silky cocoon. Still shaking with nervous energy as she attempts to free him while constantly looking over her shoulder at the massive spider.

Janet is doing her best to keep the spider's attention when she notices Lisa slowly cutting William out of his confinement. Not only did Janet notice Lisa's movement but also the spider, who quickly turns in Lisa's direction causing her to panic in fear.

"Come on woman! Get me out of here! Don't look at the spider…cut me out!" William yells.

"I don't wanna die…I don't wanna die!" Lisa nervously repeats while shaking and trying to continue cutting William out from the thick webbing.

"Hurry up woman!" said William as he is twitching attempting to free himself as Lisa continues to cut away the silky sticky webbing.

The spider is once again cleaning its mandibles while preparing to entrap Lisa in her very own silky cocoon slowly walks over in her direction.

Janet seeing the spider advance on Lisa and William looks over to Marcus as to what to do before she runs towards Lisa to block the spider's advance causing the spider to stop in its tracks.

"What are you doing crazy?" yelled Marcus at Janet.

"I don't know!" said Janet as she answers back. "Hey! Get your spider ass back over here and away from them!"

The spider once again turns its attention back to Janet. This time it swings its front left leg in Janet's direction in which she manages to avoid with an unexpected result.

Janet drops down to one knee when that eerie blue glow begins to emanate from her body once again as it did at the park. Her eyes begin to glow a burning sun yellow as her skin glows brighter and brighter with each passing second.

"Oh no. It's happening again," said Marcus with fear and concern in his voice.

Just as the spider readies itself for another attack. It quickly spins in the opposite direction towards Lisa and William completely ignoring the glowing Janet in the process. As the giant beast raises its front legs ready to strike, it lowers them as if it changed its mind.

"What the hell?" said William with a confused looked on his face.

Janet, who is now standing, still has the blue aura surrounding her body but this time she has her hand up with her palm facing the spider. The spider's eyes are now glowing a bright sun yellow just as Janet's eyes and is no longer acting in an aggressive manner.

The spider slowly begins to turn back to Janet as if in a trance before bowing down in front of Janet who proceeds to pet its head.

"That's a little freaky," said Marcus.

"Tell me about it," replied Lisa. "Is she ok?"

"At least it's no blood this time draining from her neck."

If by some psychic link, Janet raises her left hand and points towards the barrier blocking the door in which they entered to the chamber. Without hesitation, the quickly shoots a web that attaches to the barrier and begins to pull, dislodging it from its placement in the floor thus freeing the four friends from their dark and gloomy enclosure. The dark confined enclosure, which quickly became engulfed in dust, debris and dirt as the barrier came crashing down to the stone floor below causing everyone to cover their nose as well as inducing a coughing episode amongst the friends.

"Creepy but very effective," said William in-between

coughing. "At least we can get out of here now."

Janet is standing in the middle of the room with the spider as if they are a statue. Still glowing with the blue aura that caused such a concern earlier in the day. Her hand still points in the direction of the torn down barrier. The spider, whose eyes are still glowing a bright yellow, has not moved since tearing down the barrier.

Still in a little bit of shock after seeing what just happened with Janet and the spider, Marcus attempts to talk to Janet to see if he is able to reach her. As he slowly approaches her while keeping an eye on the spider at the same time. She is still glowing her bright blue aura with yellow eyes.

"Uh…Janet? You in there?" asked Marcus questionably while tiptoeing around to get face to face with her.

Janet is still motionless as Lisa and William make their way over to Marcus and Janet while also keeping their eyes on the motionless spider.

"Is she going to be ok?" asked Lisa sounding concerned.

"Yeah. Maybe she'll snap out of it like earlier…hopefully," replied Marcus.

William stands in front of Janet waving his hand in her face. "Hello. Anyone in there?"

Just as he's walking away, "I guess not." Janet lowers her arm and the spider turns to face Janet causing everyone to jump back.

"Whoa!" yelled out William.

"Knirhs won elttil dneirf. Ruoy boj si enod," muttered

Janet.

After Jane speaks that phrase of an unknown language into the world, the spider begins to decrease in size and its eyes start to lose that bright yellow color.

"Ok, this is just super freaky," said Lisa.

"Truth!" blurted out Marcus.

As fast as the spider grew in size, it was a matter of seconds before it was back down to its original size, as it was when it landed on top of the gold in front of the foursome. As it begins to scurry in Janet's direction, William attempts to stomp on it before Janet intervenes.

"Die!" yelled William.

The second William attempts to introduce the spider to the bottom of his sneaker; she once again raises her left palm towards William causing him to stop dead in his tracks. Which allows the spider to make it to Janet's leg before crawling up her body and resting on her left shoulder. Janet then lowers her hand allowing William to move again.

"What the hell woman!" yelled William.

"Chill! That is not Janet acting like this. Or are you color blind?" said Lisa.

"Whatever."

Janet lets out a creepy laugh with a smirk on her face causing William to feel creeped out on a completely new level.

"Janet!" yelled Marcus. "Come back to us!"

After a few seconds, Janet turns to Marcus just as her eyes

are returning to normal and starts to lose the blue aura surrounding her body.

"Will you stop yelling at me!"

"Janet?" questions Marcus while being cautious.

"No, I'm the school nurse. Who you think I am?"

There seems to be no ill effects that was a problem during the last incident as Janet is joking and smiling but has not noticed the spider sitting on her left shoulder.

"Um…Janet. Don't make any sudden movements or freak out but you umm…you have that killer spider on your shoulder," said Lisa.

Janet's eyes slowly begin to peel over to her left shoulder followed by her head turning just as slowly and nervously. As her head completely turns, she comes face to face with the spider who wrapped William in a web cocoon before shrugging her shoulders and acting like it's nothing there.

"Him? He is harmless. That is Red. He is the guardian of the gold," said Janet.

"Um…you know that how?" asked Lisa who is standing next to William freaked out.

"He told me so. How else would I know this?"

Everyone is staring at Janet with a blank look on their faces as to what she just said was in a foreign language. She appears normal without any ill effects of the blue aura or the burning yellow eyes. The result of a spider sitting on her shoulder does not seem to affect her mental state of affairs. Something that would freak out the sanest of people. No one is able to understand how it is that Janet knows the name of the spider or that it guards the gold. Let alone how she was able to stop William from stomping Red to death by just lifting her hand towards him.

"Do you know what just happened?" asked Lisa.

"It's a little fuzzy," replied Janet while Red just sits on her shoulder.

"You turned blue again and your eyes turned bright yellow. Hell, you even stopped William dead in his tracks just by having your palm face him," said Marcus. "On top of everything else, you got your buddy Red there to go from giant killer spider to shoulder spider just by uttering some crazy gibberish. And here we are now."

"Wow," she replied with a shocked look on her face.

"Enough with the mushy madness! We getting this gold or not?" shouted William from out the blue.

"And…he's back to normal now," said Marcus sarcastically.

Chapter Ten

All Four One

Once the friends get over the initial shock of the previous events, they continue on back to the next room with a newly acquired friend. Everyone but Janet is keeping a close watch on Red the spider in case he is secretly plotting to bite Janet or even one of them without warning.

They surround the gold as they once did before having to back away upon meeting Red the first time. This time there appears to be nothing that will stop their quest for the gold.

“Anyone notice something different this time?” asked Lisa.

“What’s up with that crazy light show?” said William. “Resident Blue Woman with the friendly gold protecting spider on her shoulder care to chime in on this situation?”

Everyone looks at Janet as if she has the right answer to that question only to receive a blank stare looking back at them as Red scurries from shoulder to shoulder.

“I still don’t see how you aren’t freaking out with a spider who just tried to eat us running around on your shoulders. Especially since you hate spiders so much,” said Lisa.

“I have no idea but I know he won’t hurt me.”

“Blah blah blah…gold here!” said William as he is pointing to the gold. “Do you not want this?”

Once again, the four surround the glittering gold that sits in the middle of the room. Each piece just glistens like a newly polished piece of metal stashed inside of a pirate style chest of the era. There is a silence in the room as they all just stand there looking into the golden light of the hidden treasure. The candles in the room remained lit just as they were when they first entered the hidden chamber.

As William stands there rubbing his hands together, a giant grin begins to spread across his face as his eyes also begin to widen. The three others look upon him in anticipation of him doing something ridiculous.

“So who wants to be in the spotlight for their fifteen minutes of agony?” asked Marcus to the rest of the group.

“Go ahead William. You want the gold so bad. Do us all a favor and show us how greedy you really are but hope you come back with all your appendages,” Janet added with a hint of sarcasm.

“I’m leaving with everything I walked in here with and a little something extra,” William replied with a more sarcastic tone while he is searching around the room for something to pierce the light encasing the gold. “Help me look for something to throw into the light.”

Everyone begins to look for any possible object that the quad of friends can throw into the light that does not involve losing an arm.

“I don’t see why we’re searching for something when we’re in an abandoned house littered with junk. Just look down and pick something up,” said Marcus.

William finds an old discarded piece of wood lying in one of the corners that was close to him about the size of a table leg. It is a little heavier than he expected, as he struggles to pick it up and place it on his shoulders, before carrying it back over and throwing it into the light surrounding the treasure trove.

"If something happens to me, I'm coming back to haunt all of you after this," said Janet as she watches the wood crash down onto the treasure trove of coins and various pieces of jewelry.

"Whatever!" said William in an even more sarcastic tone.

It would appear that even with the weight of the heavier than thought piece of wood crashing down on top of the treasure, the light not only remained intact but the treasure barely budged as it rolled off the coins hitting the floor.

"So now what? The light didn't vanish and luckily no ghost pirates," said Marcus with a sigh of relief.

"Only one thing left to do now," replied William.

Everyone pauses for a moment as they know what he is already thinking before William says another word out of his mouth.

"You're tripping!" blurted out Lisa. "No one in their right mind would even consider doing that."

"Well, it's a good thing I'm left minded," William sarcastically responds to Lisa with a big grin on his face.

It did not take long before Marcus chimed in and added his two cent into the already crazy mix of words and emotions.

"Here lies William. He got greedy and was killed by the ghost of Red Point the murderous pirate and his scallywag crew of misfits."

"Funny."

Everyone is just standing around the treasure eyeballing William to see what crazy move he intends to make now. Red, Janet's eight-legged friend, is sitting on her shoulder and is intently waiting to see what happens next.

"Doesn't it feel weird that you have a spider just sitting on your shoulder? That would so creep me out," asked Lisa.

"Trust me, he's friendly enough. No need to worry about him."

"Yeah. Until he, she, or it decides to wrap you in a cocoon and have you for dinner later," said William.

"Oh shut up Gold Fever," replied Janet.

The two continue going back and forth before they start to refocus on the treasure. William goes back to staring at the treasure while Janet begins to pace back and forth inside the tiny back hidden room. After the forth time of Janet walking past the treasure, Red decides to shimmy down off her shoulder and jumps on top of the coins.

"Now…now kiddies. Let's all behave now," said Marcus.

"Red!" yelled out Janet.

Everyone turns around to see why Janet is yelling out to see Red sitting on top of the open treasure chest scurrying around from side to side.

"Well, Red appears to be fine but then again…Red isn't a normal spider," said Marcus.

Unlike their first introduction to Red when he jumped into the light, the spider is not growing in size nor appears that the light is affecting its body. Red suddenly just stops near the left side of the treasure chest and just sits there.

"He appears to be fine. Maybe if someone takes something a la Indiana Jones style that something bad will happen. I'm not in the mood to start running from a big ass boulder," said Lisa.

"That's a possibility," said Marcus.

"I'm going in," said William feverishly with wide eyes and a glazed over look in them.

As William prepares to psyche himself up to grab a piece of gold, his heart starts racing and his body starts shaking. He begins talking to himself while pacing back in forth in front of the treasure chest.

As William takes a deep breath before proceeding to stand in front of the chest. He slowly lifts his right hand, which is noticeably shaking badly, inching it forward towards the bright light that encompasses the treasure chest.

"WILLIAM!" Marcus blurted out causing William to jump back in terror and everyone starts laughing so hard.

"What is wrong with you? You can't be scaring me half to death like that man."

"Just checking on you."

"Now shut up and let me do this."

William refocuses himself before attempting to take a piece of the treasure. He raises his right hand once again, still shaking just as much as his first attempt. Inching closer and closer before pulling his hand back and raising his left one instead.

"No. I'm right handed. No way I'm losing the hand I write with."

"Yeah, you can't lose your girlfriend being greedy," laughed Janet while making fun of William.

"Shut up!"

William rubs his hands together while biting his bottom lip before proceeding to pass through the beam of light. He slowly moves his left hand forward towards the light with his hand noticeably shaking more and more the closer he gets.

As the tip of his middle finger slightly pierces the light surrounding the treasure, he jumps back in pain, causing Red to quickly jump onto William's hand and scurrying up his arm before he pulled it completely back.

"My finger! My finger! Get this spider off of me!" yelling William as he wildly flings his arm around as Red seems to hang on tightly around his forearm.

"What happened? What happened?" Lisa rushes to get that out of her mouth while sounding worried at the same time.

Janet walks over to a crazed William to get Red off his forearm before he manages to swat him away into a wall.

"Keep still you big baby, so I can take Red off of you without him biting you. I'm surprised he didn't already after the way you're acting."

"Leave it up to you to act like a little baby," Marcus says while laughing so hard at William.

"You're not the one this stupid spider tried to eat ten seconds ago!"

"Keep still!" Janet yells at William.

After several seconds of William running around the tiny

room and flinging his arms all around, Janet manages to get Red safely off William's arm. Never did she ever see this side of William freaking out so badly. It is as if spiders were his phobia and having Red jump on his arm severely bought out his worst fear come to life. He is usually the one acting like the tough guy in the crowd when trouble starts anywhere near his girlfriend; the valiant protector, that is until a spider hops onto his arm.

"How's your finger?" Lisa asked with a scared tone to her voice as she goes to hug William.

Looking over his index finger to see how severe the burning sensation is on his skin. Flexing and gently rubbing the tip of his index in an attempt to soothe the pain and thumping feeling.

"I'm ok. It just stings a little bit. Nothing damaged," said William while Lisa hugs him tight.

"So now what are we going to do? The light cannot be broken, Red walks through undamaged, William almost lost a finger and the treasure is laughing at us if it could," Marcus says sounding frustrated. "And I'm out of ideas!"

After checking on William to make sure he is doing ok, the four gather around the shielded treasure in hopes of coming up with a new plan. As things are going right now, it seems like a longshot before they come up with any plausible way to plunder the treasure and become rich beyond their dreams.

"Any suggestions?" asked William as he is still nursing his sore finger.

Everyone just looks at each other with a blank stare before going back to pacing around the treasure chest as if they are moths attracted to the light.

"Well. We do know that inanimate objects can pass through

the light with no problem but the gold does not move an inch when struck with said object. Red can freely walk around on top of the treasure considering he, she, it was the guardian at the time we appeared. Somehow, in some crazy way, Janet was able to stop Red from putting William on the dinner menu and not only tame him but get his size to revert back to normal all the while giving off some blue aura," said Marcus. "Especially when this was not the first time this has happened since our little adventure begun."

"Question is though. How have I been able to do that and not know how I managed to do that?" Janet asked while looking puzzled and with her arms folded.

"Good question."

"Very creepy that's for sure," added Lisa. "Especially when that blue glow covers your body and you start with that ghostly power craziness."

"The thing is, I don't even feel anything when you say that is happening to me. Nor do I remember anything."

Janet now starts feeling down about her current situation not knowing what to do. She slowly backs away from the light shielded treasure and goes into one of upper right corner of the room before squatting down as to not sit on the webbing while placing her hands on her head.

Her three friends just look at her in shock, as it appears to them that she has just given up on this adventure and is admitting defeat. Not that they know how it feels to have a ghostly aura possessing their body while not remembering what happened to them in the process.

Lisa walking over to Janet before giving her a hug. "Don't worry about this, we'll figure out what's going on and then we'll be home in no time."

For a split second, Lisa manages to forget that Red was sitting on Janet's shoulder until he crawls back up from her lower back, to where he moved just before Lisa's hug. Upon seeing Red scurry back up onto Janet's shoulder after the hug caused Lisa to jump back in surprise and let out a scream.

"What is wrong with you woman?" William yelled out after seeing Lisa jump back and scream.

"R-Red just scared the hell out of me."

"Ooookaaay," William says in a long and sarcastic tone. "How you feeling Janet?"

"I'm ok. Just a little shook up about everything. I'll be fine. This is weird and creepy even by my standards."

Marcus, walking around the treasure as if it was a dying animal and he was the vulture waiting for his prey to die, begins to mumble under his breath to himself.

"So how do we get the gold past a barrier that we can't even get through?"

"What did you say?" William blurted out as he watches Marcus as he continues to circle around the treasure.

"Nothing. Just thinking out loud."

Just then, Janet gets up after dusting herself off and proceeds to talk over towards Marcus and the treasure. With every step closer towards the sacred treasure, Red begins to scurry back and forth along Janet's shoulders. After a few seconds, Lisa takes notice of this and just watches Red run back and forth several times before saying anything to everyone.

"What is going on with Red, Janet?

Janet stops suddenly just in front of the treasure causing Marcus to stop seconds before running into her.

"Yooo!"

Janet just blankly stares directly at the treasure while seemingly ignoring the question asked by Lisa. As if something out of a scary movie, she turns her head to the left slowly and then to the right before lifting her right hand palm facing the light chest high and parallel to the light that guards the treasure.

Marcus, Lisa and William are just staring at Janet with a look of not only concern but also one with lots of questions to ask. She slowly begins to press the palm of her hand into the light with a little resistance. The light begins to flicker around the shape of her hand as if a distortion in a force field is occurring. She presses harder into the light with no sense of pain on her face.

"How is that even possible? My finger was feeling like it was on fire the second I touched the light. She doesn't even looked phased," William said in a shocked tone while just watching the events unfold.

Just then, Janet pushes through the light and is within inches of being able to grab one of the forbidden coins, when her hand up to her wrist suddenly turns to bone.

"What the hell?" Marcus yelled out. "Get her out of there!"

Marcus was no more than three steps away before Janet stuck her hand into the light. Just as he begins to run to pull her out, Janet raises her left arm and stops him in his tracks.

"Not again," Lisa says in a scared tone.

The more that Janet reaches into the light, the more of her arm turns to bone.

"How is this even possible? She's not glowing, her eyes aren't a different color and she apparently isn't showing any signs of pain," William said in amazement.

"Unreal," Lisa said.

The three are helpless to do anything to help Janet in her current predicament. All they can do is watch, hope everything turns out okay and back to normal real soon.

"I wish I could move," Marcus said, as he remains paralyzed by Janet's mysterious powers.

In that same instant, Janet quickly lowers her left arm with her palm facing Marcus to her side, thus releasing him from his paralyzed state. With her right arm still deep into the light just hovering above the highest piece of gold in the chest, arm still looking as though it was skinned at her bicep to reveal only the bone. It's as if she is patiently waiting for a command in order to react to her current situation.

Suddenly, Janet lets out an eardrum-popping scream that causes everyone to jump back out of fear and surprise. The three friends cover their ears to the deafening sound as Janet screeches loudly but only for a few seconds.

"What the hell was that?" Marcus shouted while rubbing his ears to make sure he can still hear normally.

"She's changing again!" Lisa shouted in a terrified tone.

Janet begins to show signs of the transformation when Marcus attempts to grab ahold of her arm.

"Snap out of it, Janet!" Marcus yells while grabbing Janet's arm before quickly letting go just as fast. "Oww! Her skin feels like it's boiling!"

"What?" Lisa and William both yelled out at the same time while looking confused.

Janet's body is starting to glow brighter as she is now emitting enough light to illuminate the tiny secret room. She lets out another violent deafening scream that last only a few seconds but is enough to make her three friends drop to their knees while covering their ears.

"What in the h-hell is going on with her?" Marcus yelled while keeping his hands over his ears.

"What?" William replied. "I can't hear anything."

Janet's illumination is getting brighter and begins to pulsate every two seconds creating a slow strobe light effect in the tiny web filled room.

"Wow. Never would have thought that she would end up doing that," Lisa said while shielding her eyes from the bright flashing light emanating from Janet.

"This has to end now! Who knows how this is affecting her," Marcus said while trying to stand.

As fast as Janet started pulsating, she is slowly returning to normal and losing her glowing blue aura that surrounded her body. However, her arm remains in the light still appearing to be nothing but bone just above the golden coins and sparkling jewels.

"Good to see that didn't last long," Lisa said while picking herself off the sticky web covered floor.

"Hopefully she doesn't still feel like her skin is boiling and we can try to snap her out of this trance," Marcus said. "It's time to get out of here."

"Snap out of it, Janet! We want to go home!" Lisa says with tears running down her face.

Janet suddenly turns her head in Lisa's direction and her eyes flare up a dark blue causing Lisa to lean back in terror. She then slowly turns her head back towards the treasure and remains still with her right arm still hovering above the lost treasure.

"Grab her!" William yells out while running towards Janet. As with Marcus's attempt, Janet once again raises her left arm while twisting her body towards William to stop him in his tracks. "Ugh! Not this again."

"Oh no!" Lisa shouted out.

Janet closes her left hand into a fist while bending her arm so that her fist is pointing towards the ceiling. If by some invisible rope, William begins moving towards the treasure despite him leaning back and trying to dig his sneakers into the dusty spider web covered floor to slow his movement.

"What is going on?" William yelled.

"Looks like she's dragging you over to her but I may be wrong. I'm just saying," Marcus says in a sarcastic tone.

"Shut up and get me loose!"

William is within feet of Janet while he's still struggling to find a way to stop his movement and break away from whatever control Janet has over him. Janet slowly opens her left closed fist that pulled William close to her, causing him to stop moving completely inches from the treasure.

"N-now what's going to happen?"

Janet begins moving her right arm down towards the treasure while everyone just watching everything unfold. She grabs one of the coins from the top of the pile and slowly pulling her arm out from the light causing her arm to go from bone back to flesh. Red is just resting on her right shoulder as Janet pulls the coin from the light.

"I guess it's not an Indy trap," Marcus said sarcastically. "Guess you can't believe everything you see in movies."

Janet turns to William slowly with the coin in hand. "Open your hand," she says in a ghostly voice.

William is hesitant and shaking nervously as he just stares at Janet and the coin in her hand. Not knowing what will happen if he were to resist, he nervously holds out his open hand towards Janet.

William's heart is beating out of his chest as he breathes harder and harder with each breath not know what is about to happen next to him as Janet continues to hold the mystical grip on him. Janet begins to hold the coin over his open hand before quickly dropping it into his hand. No sooner than the coin leaves her hand that, she snaps out of the ghostly trance as the grip on William releases.

"W-What is going on?" said Janet.

"You were glowing again," said Marcus.

William, still gripped by fear and not realizing that he is in fact holding a piece of the sacred treasure in the palm of his hand, stands there motionless.

"Earth to Will. You in there homie?" Marcus asked while

waving his hand in front of William's face.

After several more seconds, William starts laughing lightly before it starts to get louder and more obnoxious as he begins to move. Realizing what he is now holding in his hand, his eyes begin to get wider and wider with a smile forming on his face.

"D-do you realize what I'm holding right now?" William said as excited as a kid in a candy store was with unlimited free access.

"Well, he appears to be back to his old self," said Marcus.

Janet is still a little dazed and confused while looking at William in total surprise but before she could even question how William was even holding a piece of the sacred treasure; the creepy blue aura appears around the gold along with a dense cold breeze begins blowing through the tiny hidden cobweb filled room.

"What is going on?" Lisa said in a terrified tone.

"I think we're about to have company and that it may be time to go. Like right NOW!" Marcus yelled out to everyone.

The room begins to get colder when suddenly the candles in the room go completely out as the intense cold and darkness stops the four friends dead in their tracks. Only the blue aura from the treasure dimly lights the hidden room.

"We need to get out of here!" Lisa screams in a panic state.

A low eerie noise begins to echo in the tiny room. That which sounds like mumbled voices and chains dragging on the ground slowly begin to get louder with each passing second. William now realizing what is going on after snapping out of his gold fever induced trance, begins to panic about the situation at hand.

"Let's go man! We have to get out of here!" Marcus shouts at William who he can barely see in the room. "Head for the door!"

"My flashlight is dead," Lisa shouts while smacking it with her hand a couple of times. "I can't see where I'm going."

"Mines too!" Janet replied with anger and still feeling a little woozy.

"It's enough light emanating from the treasure for us to find the door. Now grab a shoulder and let's get out of here!" Marcus shouted.

The four slowly start moving towards the door as the room begins to shake violently causing them to lose their balance and try to brace themselves as they are walking to escape the hidden enclosure. As they make it to the door, the floor begins to illuminate the cobweb covered dingy floor with a bright blue aura with each step the friends take on their way to the exit. The rumblings of voices are growing louder while the sounds of dragging chains is starting to become deafening.

Marcus now standing by the door ushering everyone out of the room in a hastily manner, is suddenly and forcefully pushed out of the room onto the cold stone floor on the opposite side of the hidden room, as soon as Lisa, the last one out crosses through the doorway.

"Ahhhhhh!"

Everyone stops in their tracks to turn around to see Marcus slowly picking himself up from the cold floor after forcibly being pushed from the hidden room onto the cold slimy stone floor.

Chapter Eleven

All That Remains

The unseen force easily pushed Marcus five feet out of the room with little effort causing him to land on his right shoulder first slamming onto the stone. When Marcus looks back at the door to see what pushed him out, he sees only a blue outline of what looks like a ghost pirate staring directly at him with red eyes glowing standing in the doorway.

"We have to go…NOW!" Marcus shouted to everyone while holding his shoulder. "Run! Get to the rope bridge!"

Janet runs back to Marcus to check on him and to help him get going. As she's helping him up, she looks over at the door and pauses for a second. She too sees the red eyes staring back at her and she gets a chill over her body before turning to run with Marcus towards the rope bridge to escape the house.

Suddenly a loud moaning scream comes from the direction of the hidden room, which causes the interior of the house to shake. Dust and loose debris start to fall from the ceiling of the basement compartment while the four friends make their way to the rope bridge.

"I-I am never going out with you to something this crazy again William!" Lisa yells while running as fast and cautiously as she can.

"Worry about that later. Get across the bridge!" William replied quickly.

"Is it me or have we been running forever? This path was never this long when we first came down here," Marcus said while holding his bruised and throbbing shoulder.

"Are we even in the same place? This looks so different," said Lisa while trying to turn on her flashlight. "Lights are still not working."

"Great," said Janet with a loud sigh.

Suddenly the four hear a loud rumbling coming from behind them as they all stand still anticipating what is coming for them.

From out of nowhere, an enormous thump shakes the stone floor as if a giant were walking towards them in a slow forceful manner.

"What the hell was that?" William yelled while trying to maintain his balance after the sudden shakeup.

Another even stronger thump rattles the lower basement level harder than the last. This time a loud slow moaning voice echoes through the dark damp corridor.

"Give…me…my…gold!" The eerie voice proclaimed. Freaking out the four friends who then began to huddle up against one another.

"Did you hear that or am I losing my mind?" Lisa asked in a very terrified tone.

"I wish I didn't," said Janet. "This is your fault William. If you didn't have gold fever…we wouldn't be here."

"Whatever!"

Another loud thump is heard again before a giant

shockwave is felt causing the stone flooring to shake violently. The affect causes the gang of four to sway from side to side with their arms out to the side to maintain their balance and not fall over.

"That was a big one. We need to get out of here," said Marcus.

"Just give them back their gold," shouted Lisa who is already severely terrified by the events of tonight.

"NO!" William yelled back. "Blame Janet for this situation. Her ass is the one who turned blue and pulled me towards her. Or did we all just forget that little tidbit of information."

"Shut up!" Janet yelled back.

Again, the four friends hear the eerie voice demanding the return of its gold except this time, a giant blast of cold air forcefully pushes them farther up the corridor in which they were running.

"We gotta get out of here," said Marcus as he pulls up the rear of the four friends.

"You're a genius," replied William with every ounce of sarcasm he could muster. "Why didn't we think of that?"

Seeming to run for blocks and blocks down the never-ending corridor, the unsteady rope bridge finally comes into view.

"I can see the bridge," an overly excited yet terrified Lisa blurts out.

They arrive finally to the unstable bridge out of breath and gasping for air with racing heartbeats that sound like band drums thumping out of their chests.

"Hurry up and get across!" Janet yelled out, as Lisa is the

first to touch the bridge's wobbly structure causing everyone to fall in line behind her.

Lisa slowly places her right foot on the first plank of the unsteady bridge before bearing her full weight and placing her left foot onto the next one. The plank begins to squeak as Lisa begins placing more weight on it causing Lisa to jump back in fear of it breaking on her.

Another loud thump is heard, shaking the ground beneath their feet and making the bridge sway heavily from side to side. More debris begins falling from the ceiling of the hidden passage raining down on the four friends.

"Cover your head!" Marcus yelled out.

William pushes his way to the front of Janet and Lisa so he can attempt to cross the bridge to escape the creepy house with his treasure in hand.

"Outta the way. Real man coming through. It's time to get out of here in one piece and I'm about to be rich."

"Well let me know when he gets here," replied Janet.

Janet and William begin to eyeball each other down before Lisa steps in to break up the commotion. "Can we do this after we get out of here? We do have a ghost pirate chasing us."

Before the two can regain their focus on getting across the bridge, another shockwave rumbles through the area followed by the ghostly voice demanding their gold back. At the same time, the long corridor in which they just ran through is becoming brighter and brighter with each passing second.

"I suggest we get moving. Let's go William!" Marcus calmly but urgently said to everyone.

William slowly starts making his way onto and across the rope and blank bridge followed closely by Lisa then Janet with Marcus at the rear. With each step they take, the planks squeak and screech as if they are about to break.

The gang is taking a slow and steady approach to crossing the bridge despite a ghostly presence surrounding them. The blue aura of light finally reaches the bridge and stops just as Marcus is stepping onto the third plank while he's looking back in shock.

"GO! GO! GO!" Marcus yells as he feels the cold air on the back of his neck. "It's getting a little uncomfortable back here."

Step by step and creeky screeching plank by plank, the four friends slowly make their way across the unstable bridge. Each plank feels as though they are going to break under the weight of each footstep. With every squeak and cracking of the plank, Lisa gets more nervous and anxious to reach the other side safely. The blue aura that chased after them sits idle at the beginning of the rope bridge pulsating quickly with a slow pause after each burst of light.

"I don't like the looks of that," Marcus said as he looks back at the ghostly aura that was once breathing down the back of his neck.

"At least it hasn't moved since we got on this bridge and let's hope it doesn't," replied Janet.

Nearly halfway across the bridge, a strong cold wind blows across their body and forcefully shakes the unstable bridge.

Once again, the ghostly voice echoes through the corridor demanding back what was recently stolen from their hidden bounty.

"Hang on everyone! We're almost there," said Janet.

"Imma be rich! Imma be rich! Just as soon as I get out of here," William mumbles to himself but was overheard by Lisa.

"And you better give me some of that money after all of this insanity."

"You know I got you baby."

No sooner and within feet of crossing the bridge, Red Point himself appears in front of the four friends, causing William to stop dead in his tracks and Lisa running into the back of him.

"What the hell William? Why'd you stop?" Lisa questioning his decision to stop short.

"Why does something smell burnt?" questioned Marcus as he is not paying attention since he is looking back at the blue aura and runs into the back of Janet.

Janet turns around and shoots Marcus the evil eye of disgust.

"Excuse you."

"My bad Janet but what's the hold up about up there?"

Not wanting to be the bearer of bad news but William as calmly as he can describes the situation in front of him.

"Guys. We have a major situation up here," William said but no sooner than he is finishing his sentence, the whole corridor explodes in a flash of bright blue light.

"My eyes," William cried out.

The four friends attempt to shield their eyes from the flash but to no avail. The light is so intense that all they could manage was to turn their back and squat down behind each other.

“Give…me…my…gold!” The ghostly voice demanded as the intense blue aura starts to fade away slowly.

“Give them back that coin fool!” Marcus yells at William as he slowly uncovers his eyes. “Hmm, the light is fading.”

As William goes to stand up and turn around, he turns right into a face-to-face meeting with Red Point. An event that made him stumble backwards onto his hands that caused his left arm to go off the left side of a bridge plank, nearly sending him over the edge.

Lisa grabs William before he tumbles over the edge. “Get your butt back here.”

“That would explain the stoppage,” said Marcus. “That must be Red Point. I’m guessing he’s seen better less toasty days,” Marcus sarcastically says. “And his little lackeys too.”

Janet cannot help but turn around and give Marcus the evil eye once again. “Now you want to be sarcastic?”

“What? Someone’s gotta be.”

Red Point has the same blue aura that surrounds Janet when she is possessed by some unseen force. He looks to be six feet five, his face is over eight percent severely burned with his left side of his jaw down around his mouth is just melted away exposing is skeletal remains and one burned upper left front gold tooth. On his head lies a burned captain’s hat with a jewel in the center, a red burned and tattered jacket with a burned shirt ripped diagonally from right to left going upward. His hands are dripping with burned rotted flesh picked apart by the various birds in the area of where his body was dumped after his execution. Tattered what appears to be black pants with burn holes that expose decaying flesh and his skeletal remains of his legs. Red Point, flanked by two slim shadowy figures with glowing red eyes.

"Someone needs some sun tan lotion," Marcus sarcastically blurts out.

"Really!" Janet yelled out.

"Not my fault he was hung then was apparently burnt."

Red Point and his two lackeys begin to circle around the gang on the bridge leaving a blue aura trail behind them as they pass. The blue aura crackles and appears to burn in place as Red Point circles them in anticipation.

"What is going on?" said Lisa.

"That looks like the same light that was surrounding the treasure," said William.

"Try not to touch it this time. You might get more than a sting," Lisa said nervously while watching Red Point circle around them.

The friends are so close to each other that Janet and Lisa are almost sandwiched in the middle of the four. They hear a low mumbling as Red Point continues to circle them, which no one can decipher. As if someone was slowly turning the volume up on the remote, the mumblings begin to get louder and louder.

"Give…me…my…gold!" as Red Point continues circling the friends. With each spoken word, the cavern around the bridge begins to shake.

"It's time to do something. I refuse to be a dead pirate's roasted human marshmallow," Marcus sarcastically blurted out.

"What are we going to do?" asked Lisa in a more terrified tone as Red Point circles closer to her.

Janet slides her way to the front of the pack to come within inches of the blue aura of light.

"What are you doing?" Marcus yelled out.

Suddenly Red Point comes crashing through the blue aura and is face to face with Janet. A sudden move that made her jump back in surprise.

Red Point and his lackeys are just staring Janet down as they move from side to side giving her the once over.

Suddenly Red Point lets out a high pitch scream that instantly made the four friends cover their ears in agony and drop down to their knees.

"MY…GOLD!" Red Point yelled out.
"Give…Me…My…Gold!"

Red Point's hot decaying breaths is blowing right in Janet's face as he yells for his gold to be returned to him. Not being able to take the smell of decaying burnt breaths blowing on her face any longer, Janet slowly rises to her feet, while still covering her ears. She lets out a deafening scream of her own to the likes of which Red Point was not prepared to handle. Such a scream pushed Red Point and his shadow minions back as the scream contained a blue aura of its own coming from Janet's mouth.

"What in the hell?" William says in amazement and surprise.

"She Godzilla'd his ass!" Marcus shouted.

Janet slowly begins to take on her blue aura as she sees Red Point backing away in surprise as to what is going on. She raises her right hand to the blue barrier and with one touch of her palm, forming an opening big enough for them to run through.

"GO! NOW!" shouted the possessed ghostly form of Janet.

"You don't have to tell me twice," said William as he begins to run through the opening carefully while being on the bridge.

"NOOOO!" shouted Red Point as he came rushing back to the four friends.

Just as his decrepit hand is within inches of grabbing William by the neck, Janet lifts her left hand stopping Red Point in his tracks.

"WOOOW," the three let out a collective emotion at once while running as quickly as they could over the bridge to the other side.

Janet is now straining to control Red Point from advancing as she makes her way across the bridge to the where her friends are.

"G...Grannn," shouted Red Point.

"Let's go Janet!" Marcus yells out as he looks back to see where she was.

Red Point is slowly gaining ground on Janet as she is struggling to keep him at bay long enough for the others to escape.

"Just run Janet! Lisa and William are already heading for the steps."

Janet finally breaks the hold on Red Point, who at this point is furious, as Janet reaches the other side with Marcus.

Marcus helps a stumbling Janet get to her feet as he throws her right arm around his neck as he holds her around the waist.

"You can do this Janet. We gotta get going. I think you pissed him off."

"I feel so…weak."

"Well you're about to feel nothing if Red Point catches us."

The two make haste for the stone stairs with Red Point hot on their tails. As they get three steps up the staircase, the walls start crumbling in on them and the steps begin to crumble to pieces to the cavern below with each step.

"GO…GO…GO! I'm not trying to die in some old building!" Marcus yelled out to Janet.

The whole area is lit up in a bright blue light as Red Point chases after the gang of four to get his missing gold back from them.

Lisa and William are already at the top of the stone stairs standing by the old wooden door they struggled to reopen while waiting for Janet and Marcus to reach them.

"Come on you two! Hurry up!" William yelled to Janet and Marcus.

Just as they are approaching the door, Red Point disappears and the door slowly begins to close on Janet and Marcus as the steps behind them continue to crumble and fall to the cavern below.

"Oh no! Hold the door William!" Lisa yelled.

William attempts to brace his back against the door as he digs his sneakers into the slippery dust covered flooring.

"Will you two hurry up! I can't hold this forever."

Janet rushes through the door just as it begins to close with Marcus right behind her but the door begins to close faster, pushing William across the floor with Marcus just sliding through with inches to spare but not without Marcus' shirt snagging on the door.

"Help!" Marcus yelled. "I'm snagged on the door."

"Only you. You escape a ghost to only get snagged by a door," William responded.

"Funny."

William helps Marcus get his shirt unsnagged.

"You owe me one."

"Yeah yeah…put it on my tab. Let's just get out of here."

They hear the last of the stone landing crumble and smash along the wall as it drops into the darkness below.

"Happy I'm on this side of the door," Marcus says while huffing and puffing. "I can't wait to get home and be in my own bed."

"Hey. My flashlight is working again," Lisa said in the happiest tone since everything has happened.

"Great!" said Janet.

The four friends proceed to make their way through the abandoned house towards the front door with no signs of Red Point or his lackeys. The house is just as quiet as it was when they first entered.

As they continue through the house to get to the front door, small things seem out of place compared to the first time they walked through. All of the painting on the walls are uncovered and the eyes seem to follow the four friends throughout the room. Chairs are overturned in the middle of the rooms and hallways.

Lisa suddenly gets a chill down her body.

"Anyone else feel like we're being watched?"

"What do you expect? We are in a haunted house," said Marcus. "Of course it's going to feel like you're being watched."

A chair suddenly flies across the room from the right side as they are entering the big living room that sits right before the front door causing the four to jump back in fear crashing into the wall on the other side.

"What was that?" Lisa sounding terrified yelled out.

"Yeah! Time to go!"

The four friends are within visible range of the front door and their escape from the nightmare of this house. Just as they cross into the living room, they feel that cold ghostly blast of cold air rush over them instantly. Every piece of furniture from the previous room comes crashing behind them, blocking them from backing away and running.

"Give…me…my…gold!" Red Point's ghostly voice fills the stale quiet air that shakes the entire room.

"Just give it up William! We found the treasure and proved it's real," Lisa yelled out.

A blue fog begins to rush into the room and settle in front of the door completely blocking any escape. Red Point and his two lackeys materialize from thin air with a bright blue aura surrounding them as they hover inches above the dusty floor.

Slowly inching closer and closer to the four friends with each passing second.

Red Point holds out his right decrepit hand palm side up.

"My…gold!"

"He wants you homie," said Marcus while slapping William on the back.

William steps forward towards Red Point.

"Hell no!" said William as he proceeds to flip the bird to Red Point and his two lackeys.

The blue aura surrounding Red Point quickly turns red and the whole house begins to shake in anger.

"Look what you did now. Like we really need a pissed off poltergeist," Marcus said while backing into the furniture barricade.

"MY…GOLD!" Red Point yells while charging at the four friends with his right hand cocked back ready to strike.

Just as Red Point is ready to strike, Janet takes her possessed form again to stop Red Point from attacking. This time, her powers are not enough to stop the charging poltergeist from attacking.

Inches from attacking William, Red Point stops his attack due to focusing on something.

"G…Grand…daughter!"

"What the hell?" says Marcus as he was bracing himself for Red Point's attack.

With that break in the action, Janet manages to push William right into Red Point's reach as the two lackeys grab him.

William begins to struggle while kicking and screaming.

Next thing William knows, he's kicking and screaming in his bed as he wakes up throwing his blankets all over the place nearly falling out of bed. Blackout wakes up and rushes over to William's bedside barking.

"What just happened?" Williams says while breathing hard and finally realizing he is in his own bed. "That was a crazy ass dream."

William, after a few minutes manages to lay back down and fall back to sleep while Blackout goes back to his dog bed. After about ten minutes, Blackout's ears perked up as if he hears someone in his space. A bright blue aura slowly starts to form in William's room just inches from the front of his bed. Just off to the right of where Blackout's dog bed is located.

"Where's…my…gold…tooth?"

Red Point appears alone unexpectedly from the blue aura in search of his missing gold tooth. Within seconds, Blackout lunges at Red Point, biting him on his butt, causing Red Point to instantly disappear into thin air. Blackout barks two times before going back to his bed.

"Go to bed Blackout," William says in his sleep, not realizing what just happened, before he goes back to snoring the rest of the night.

Little did William know but Red Point's missing gold tooth sits just inches from William's alarm clock on his night stand just to the left of his bed.

Meanwhile, Lisa is awakened from her sleep by a strange scratching noise next to her bed. Thinking the noise was coming from outside from an animal running across the roof of her home, she paid it no mind seeing as though she was sleep. She didn't want to overreact and have her nerves shot. Then she suddenly heard what she thought was a coin dropping onto her nightstand to the right of her bed. She quickly jumped out of bed to turn her light on to look at her nightstand, to see the gold coin from the haunted house. On her nightstand scratched in the wood was the word, "Grannn." Lisa barely slept the rest of the night as she quickly became short of breath with a racing heart and a shaking body.

Marcus is home snug in his bed knocked out sleeping not suspecting of any of the events that transpired tonight.

Janet is also at her home sleeping in her bed as well. She slowly turns over in her sleep facing left and then to the right only to open her eyes in her sleep. Her eyes are glowing that infamous blue light before they close again.

And Red, he's somewhere possibly under someone's bed or hiding behind some old clothes in the back of a closet waiting until it will be his time to be called upon again to protect and serve.

ABOUT THE AUTHOR

Nicholas has been writing stories since the age of 13, dating back to middle school. Known for his creative writing and vivid imagination, his short stories became a source of entertainment, growing up with requests from his peers to be included into one of his many adventures. Throughout the years, he's written various stories based from sci-fi to comedy mixed with a little horror and mystery to the fantasy world. Updating old stories to the modern era at the time of revision. Thus bringing "All That Remains" to the forefront. A revised short story from seventh grade to this day and age. A long journey that finally reached the pinnacle of publication. This is just the beginning. Expect a lot more.

Made in the USA
Middletown, DE
27 August 2023